D0533998

Marcia Muller pioneered the contemporary female private investigator novel, with the first Sharon McCone mystery, *Edwin of the Iron Shoes,* in 1977. The Sharon McCone private eye series has since gained huge critical acclaim, an enormous readership, and dozens of imitators.

Marcia Muller lives in northern California, where she is working on further Sharon McCone novels.

Other Marcia Muller titles from The Women's Press:

There's Something in a Sunday (1992)
The Shape of Dread (1992)
Trophies and Dead Things (1992)
Where Echoes Live (1992)
Pennies on a Dead Woman's Eyes (1993)
Edwin of the Iron Shoes (1993)
Ask the Cards a Question (1993)
Wolf in the Shadows (1994)
Leave a Message for Willie (1994)

And the forthcoming:

Till the Butchers Cut Him Down

MARCIA MULLER

A SHARON McCONE MYSTERY

GAMES TO KEEP THE DARK AWAY

Published in Great Britain by The Women's Press Ltd, 1994
A member of the Namara Group
34 Great Sutton Street, London EC1V 0DX

First published in the United States of America by
St Martin's Press, 1984

British Library Cataloguing-in-Publication Data
A catalogue record for this book is available from the British Library

ISBN 0 7043 4368 1

Printed and bound in Great Britain by Cox & Wyman Ltd,
Reading, Berks

For my mother,
Kathryn S. Muller,
And in memory of my father,
Henry J. Muller

1

The wind whipped my jacket open as I went up to the guardrail. The sheer, rock-strewn face of Potrero Hill dropped away for fifty yards or more, and I could look down on the roofs of the houses below. I turned, pulling the jacket tightly around me, and walked down the street from where I'd parked at the dead end. Broken glass and other debris crunched beneath my feet.

All the buildings save two in this short block were condemned or half demolished. They stood silent in the early October dusk, gaping holes where windows had once been, jagged timbers silhouetted against the dying light. I shivered, only partly from the biting wind.

Number twenty-one was surrounded by a six-foot red-wood fence on which the number was spelled out in carved letters. I pushed through the gate into a deep front yard that was choked with vegetation. A gravel walk overhung by scraggly palm trees led to the front door. I went up and rang the bell.

In a moment the door opened a crack and a pale, nondescript face peered at me over the security chain. "Yes?"

"Mr. Snelling? I'm Sharon McCone, the investigator from All Souls Legal Cooperative." I passed one of my cards through the narrow opening. After a few seconds the chain rattled, the door opened, and I was admitted into a dark hallway.

The man quickly rechained the door, then turned to me, his hand outstretched. "It's good of you to come so promptly. I'm Abe Snelling."

I clasped his slender, long-fingered hand. Its palm was moist. "I'm glad to meet you. I admire your photographs."

"Thank you. Come this way." He led me down the hall toward the back of the house. So far I couldn't tell much about Snelling, except that he was short, shorter than my own five six, and that his blond hair was thinning at the crown. I followed him into a large, white-carpeted living room and stopped, caught up in the view.

In the foreground the lights of Potrero Hill cascaded down into the industrial flatlands below. The warehouses, oil storage tanks, and ships in drydock were softened by the dusk, and beyond them the water of the Bay lay flat and quiet. My gaze moved to the East Bay hills and the shining chain of bridge that linked the two shores.

"Your view of the Bay and the hills is spectacular," I said.

"Yes, I enjoy it during the day." Snelling crossed the dark room and drew the draperies with a decisive snap of the cord. He then went around flicking on table lamps. The walls of the room were also white and covered with his photographs. The furnishings were severely modern.

I must have had an odd expression on my face because Snelling stopped and gave me a lopsided grin, his head cocked to one side. "I can't stand to have the drapes open after dark."

"It *is* pretty bleak-looking out there."

"No, it's not that." He motioned at a chair. "Actually, it's snipers."

"What?"

"I have a ridiculous fear of snipers."

"Oh." I sat down in one of those chrome-and-leather chairs that are surprisingly comfortable in spite of their looks.

Snelling sat across the glass coffee table from me and fumbled in his shirt pocket for a pack of cigarettes. "It's stupid, but when I was in my teens one of the neighborhood kids shot his mother. She was standing at the kitchen window and he went out in the backyard and shot her through the glass with his hunting rifle. A thing like that makes an impression on you."

"I guess so."

"Anyway, since then, I've never been able to have the curtains open after dark. I know it's stupid, but I can't seem to help it."

"We all have those kinds of fears," I said, thinking of my own phobia about birds.

Snelling fiddled with a chrome table lighter, and I watched him, disappointed that he didn't fit my notion of what a celebrity photographer should look like. I wasn't sure exactly what I had expected, but Snelling wasn't it. He was slender, with an almost unnatural pallor and washed-out blue eyes. He wore faded jeans with a hole in one knee, a workshirt stained with darkroom chemicals, and scuffed loafers. His abrupt motions reminded me of a bird, the kind you see running along the tide line at the beach. The association did nothing to endear him to me.

Still, he was a potential client and it was time to get down to business. "Mr. Snelling, I understand you have a problem you want me to investigate."

He finally got the cigarette lit and looked up. "Yes, as I told your boss—Hank Zahn is your boss?"

I nodded.

"Well, as I told Hank Zahn, it's not the sort of thing I can go to the police about. I mean, it could be nothing and then Jane would be furious with me."

"Let's start at the beginning. Who's Jane?"

"Jane Anthony, my roommate. She's missing."

I took a pad and pencil out of my bag and noted the name. "For how long?"

"A week. Exactly a week today."

"Tell me what happened."

"There's not much to tell. I had an early-morning photo session. I do all my work in my studio, upstairs." He waved a hand at a circular stairway that ascended to a second story. "As far as I knew, Jane was still asleep in her room. The session took a long time; it was with Anna

Adams—you know, the actress who's starring in that terrible musical at the Golden Gate?"

"Yes."

"Well, Miss Adams is a good actress, but she's got the attention span of a flea. It took hours to get a few decent shots. During that time, I thought I heard Jane in the kitchen below. When Miss Adams left, Jane was also gone."

"She didn't leave a note?"

"No, nothing."

"Is she in the habit of going off without telling you?"

"Never."

"So what did you do?"

"At first I didn't think much of it. I went about my daily routine. But, when dinnertime came and went, and Jane still hadn't shown, I got worried. I called a few of her friends around nine, but they hadn't heard from her."

"What about her place of employment? Does she work?"

He shook his head. "Jane's an unemployed social worker. With all the budget cuts, jobs in that field are hard to come by."

"What did you do next?"

"Waited. Checked back with the same friends the next day. Halfway through the week I called Jane's mother—she lives down south in a coastside village called Salmon Bay, near Port San Marco. I didn't want to alarm Mrs. Anthony—she's old and not in very good health—so I just said Jane had mentioned she might stop in there on her way to L.A. But her mother hadn't heard from her."

"Did Jane take any of her things with her?"

"As far as I can tell, only enough for a night or two. Her stuff's gone from the bathroom, and there's an overnight case missing from her closet, but her big suitcases are still there."

"I assume she drove."

"Yes. She has a white . . . I think it's a Toyota, about five years old."

"Do you know the model?"

"No." He spread his hands apologetically. "I have a VW beetle and, except for that type, all cars look alike to me."

I noted the probable make and year of Jane's car. "Do you have a picture of your roommate?"

He turned and gestured to the far wall, which was covered with photographs. "The one on the extreme left."

I got up and went over to it. Jane Anthony was a strong-featured woman in her mid-thirties. Her dark hair was pulled back severely, accentuating her prominent nose and the forward thrust of her chin. It was not a pretty face, but a commanding one and, surprisingly, Snelling had made her attractive in the photo. It was not what one expected of the man who termed his work "the portraiture of realism."

I turned. "Do you have a copy that I could have?"

"Yes, upstairs." He got up and went toward the circular stairway. "I'll get one."

While he was gone, I turned back to the wall and looked at the other photos. They were by no means the pretty tinted variety you saw in the windows of ordinary photographers' studios. Instead, they were severe and uncompromisingly truthful—Snelling's trademark. I went to the opposite wall where, over the stone fireplace, I had spotted the picture that had made him famous.

It had happened only a year ago, when Abe Snelling was merely another down-at-the-heels photographer roaming San Francisco's streets in search of subjects. One morning while passing the Blue Owl Cafe, here on Potrero Hill near San Francisco General Hospital, Snelling had seen a man run out, pursued by the restaurant proprietor, a gentle soul who was well liked in the neighborhood. Sensing the unusual and obeying his photographer's instincts, Snelling readied his camera. The two men struggled, a shot was fired, the proprietor staggered and fell to the ground, and the robber ran off. As the proprietor's wife knelt over the dying man, futilely willing the life to stay in his body, Snelling snapped picture after picture of her anguished face. The photograph that he sold to the evening paper was picked up by the wire services, and eventually was featured on the cover of *Time*'s issue on crime in the cities.

It was a grisly beginning, but Snelling's career had bourgeoned after that, and now he was the "in" photographer of a wealthy and famous clientele. Society people and celebrities were all eager to expose themselves to the harsh eye of Snelling's camera; maybe they found it refreshing to see themselves with none of the warts removed.

Now I stepped back and looked at the photo from a distance. An amateur photographer myself, I liked to think I was some judge of the art and, if I knew anything at all, the actual picture seemed strangely diminished compared to the reproductions I'd seen. It was as if the starkness of the surrounding white-on-white decor had leeched away all its rich emotion, leaving only a caricature in place of the anguished woman.

Snelling clattered down the spiral staircase and extended a five-by-seven copy of Jane Anthony's picture to me. I slipped it into my bag and said, "I'd like to see Jane's room if I may."

He nodded and took me to a second stairway that led downstairs; as in many of San Francisco's hillside houses, the bedrooms were on the lower level. Jane's room was at the end of the hall. Snelling pushed the door open and motioned me in.

The first thing that struck me was the room's extreme tidiness. I myself am a finicky housekeeper—I have to be, living in a studio apartment with all my worldly goods—but this room bore the mark of a fanatic. The double bed would have passed a military inspection; perfume bottles, comb, brush, and mirror were perfectly aligned on the dresser; the spines of the books in the bookcase were straight and an exact inch from the edge of the shelf; even the wastebasket had been emptied. I went to the closet and found what I had expected—a row of skirts, blouses, dresses, and pants arranged by color and type. Shoes were lined up in a rack on the floor.

I turned to Snelling. "Mr. Snelling—"

"Abe, please."

"Abe, let me ask you this—what is the relationship between you and Jane?"

"I don't follow you."

"Were you just roommates or . . ."

"Oh. Just roommates. I met Jane a couple of months after she moved here from Salmon Bay. She has an interest in photography, so we hit it off right away. She'd hoped to get a job as a social worker but, like I said, they're hard to come by. I felt sorry for her—she was working part-time as a typist and having trouble paying her rent—so I suggested she move in here until a decent job came along. Of course, I never realized she'd be with me for six months."

"I see."

"Not that I mind having her here," he added quickly. "She's quiet and considerate—and a good cook."

I went to the bookshelf. There were textbooks—some of which I recognized from my days as a sociology major—and popular self-help manuals and a great deal of paperback science fiction. Taking a book out, I saw that it had been read, but carefully, without cracking the spine. I then went through the dresser and bedside table drawers. They were as precisely arranged as everything else—and devoid of anything personal.

"What about these friends you checked with?" I asked Snelling. "When did you last contact them?"

"This morning. They still hadn't heard from Jane."

"Do you know if she kept an address book?"

"A small one, in her purse. I looked for it, but obviously she took it with her."

"Can you think of anywhere else she might have noted things, like appointments or names and addresses?"

He frowned. "Maybe in the front of the phone book. She scribbled things down in there sometimes."

I had noticed a directory on the bottom shelf of the

bedside table. Pulling it out, I turned to the front pages. There, in a bold hand that fit with the woman in Snelling's photograph, were various notations—*Gold Mirror, 18th & Taraval . . . 43 Masonic bus (to Geary) . . . SFG Pharmacy 12–8 . . . Kelly Services, Market near 6th . . . Cannery Cinema, cheap show Wed* . . . The notations seemed to be the names of restaurants, shops, theaters, and bus routes, merely the details of daily life in the city.

I closed the phone book and replaced it, unconsciously lining it up with the shelf edge in much the way its owner would have. Then I turned to the window and looked out over the darkening vista of vacant lots and half-demolished houses. As before, I shivered.

"Pretty desolate, isn't it?" Snelling said from the doorway. He hadn't ventured into the room, presumably because of the phantom snipers beyond the open draperies.

"I noticed the demolition, of course. It strikes me as a lonely place to live."

"Maybe, but this part of Potrero Hill has the best weather in the city. Since I work only with natural light, good weather is important. Besides, it won't be lonely for long. Those houses are being torn down to make way for a condominium complex; they're building them all over the hill. I'm sorry about that, because I like the solitude."

I had heard that Snelling was quite a recluse. In spite of his celebrity, the shy photographer was never photographed himself and even refused to attend exhibitions of his own work. It was said that he ventured out of his house less and less these days, insisting his clients come to his studio here rather than go to them.

I continued gazing at the view, wondering where to start looking for Jane Anthony on the basis of the few facts I had, until I heard Snelling shuffle his feet. He was still nervous about snipers, even if I wasn't. I took a final look around the room and then followed him back upstairs.

"Are you sure you don't want to bring the police in on this, Abe?" I asked.

"No!" He looked surprised at the violence of his own answer, then repeated more softly, "No. If Jane has just gone off for some private reason, she'll be furious with me."

He seemed excessively concerned with Jane's temper. "She *did* go off without telling you."

"I know, but she'd say she's an adult and entitled to live her own life. Please, Sharon, can't you find her without involving the police?"

"I'll try." I asked him for the names of the friends he'd contacted as well as Jane's mother's phone number and address in Salmon Bay. He got an address book and read them off to me.

"Do you plan to talk to Mrs. Anthony?" he asked as he followed me down the hall to the door.

"It's a good place to start. I'll try not to alarm her. But, frankly, there's so little of your roommate here—nothing personal at all—that I really don't have any sense of who she is or what she's likely to do."

"Funny." He paused, his hand on the doorknob. "I thought I knew her, but I don't have any sense of that either."

"Well, maybe her mother will fill me in."

"Maybe." But he sounded doubtful.

We said good-night and I went out into the crisp fall evening. As I started down the overgrown path, I heard Snelling chain the door and lock himself securely into his sanctuary.

2

As I walked back to my car I noticed a black VW parked nearby. It hadn't been there before and, since it was even more beat-up than my own MG, I wondered if its owner had abandoned it. My question was answered when I drove off. The VW's lights flashed on and it pulled out after me.

I turned off of Snelling's street onto Missouri, heading for home, but I wasn't very familiar with Potrero Hill and I quickly found that it had any number of streets that came to dead ends. In the dark I lost my bearings and, at the same time, I became conscious that the same set of headlights had been shining in my rearview mirror for quite a while. They were small and close-set, and I wondered if it could be the VW I'd seen near Snelling's house and, if so, why it was following me. Possibly it had something to do with my visit to the photographer but more likely it was someone who had spotted me, a woman alone, and decided to play games. The best course of action was to get off this damned hill; I could lose him on the flatlands.

I came to Twentieth and went left. It was a through street, but it curved back, taking me even farther out of my way. Irritated, I jammed on my brakes and made a U-turn, my headlights illuminating a rustic board fence that surrounded one of the communal gardens that dotted the area's vacant lots. As I went back up the rise, the old black car passed me. I tried to get a glimpse of the driver, but his headlights blinded me. When I reached Vermont Street I stopped, waiting to see if he would keep going or turn.

He made a U at the same spot in the curve as I had, then started back up. I put my car in gear and went right on Vermont, deciding to give this business the acid test. Ahead was the section known as "the second most crooked street in the world"—a series of esses actually more perilous than the famous Lombard Street on Russian Hill. I left the MG in first gear and snaked down between the concrete embankments, past a cypress-dotted park on one side and the brightly lit windows of houses and apartment buildings on the other. At first I thought the other car had given up, but as I hit the straightaway and put on speed, I spotted its lights.

In my years as a private detective, I'd tailed people and had been tailed in return, but I'd never experienced anything like this. It was the most amateurish job I'd ever seen. My inclination was to suspect kids playing a prank—but kids were never this persistent. If it was someone following me because of my visit to Abe Snelling,

I wanted to get a look at him. I slowed and turned in front of S.F. General Hospital. When I looked back, my pursuer was gone.

I didn't know whether to be disappointed or relieved. Downshifting, I stopped for a light in front of the old red brick buildings of the hospital. To my left was the Blue Owl Cafe, scene of Snelling's photographic triumph. Its windows were dark, the umbrellas on the little outdoor tables furled. The entire neighborhood had a quiet, shut-down appearance. Even the wails of ambulances were momentarily stilled. I gave the iron gates of the hospital a cursory glance, then did a double take. The black car waited just inside one of the auto entrances. Obviously its driver had known some shortcut through the hospital grounds. The light changed and I gunned the MG straight ahead. My pursuer pulled out of the driveway and careened across three lanes of traffic after me.

What now? I asked myself.

The amateurishness of the tail job had convinced me the driver couldn't possibly be much of a threat—and that in itself could be dangerous. For safety's sake, I decided to lead him to my own neighborhood.

When I reached my own block on Guerrero Street, I began to look for a parking space. I left the first one I found for my pursuer and took one closer to my apartment building. When I saw him slip into the space, I got out of my car, locked it, and glanced back. I still couldn't see the driver through the glare of the headlights. I walked down the sidewalk, past my building, and glanced back again. A woman of about my height was getting out of the other car. In seconds, footsteps tapped behind me. I turned and ran up the outside steps of the building three doors down from mine, then flattened myself against the wall by the mailboxes inside the dark entrance.

The woman's footsteps faltered and stopped just short of the entrance. I waited, barely breathing. When the footsteps started again, they seemed to be going away. Once more they stopped, then came back toward me with renewed speed. A figure came through the archway and ran up the steps.

She was slender, dressed in a corduroy jacket and jeans. In the dark, she missed seeing me. She had her back to me, scanning the doorbell buzzers on the opposite wall, when I stepped forward and said, "Okay, what do you want?"

The woman gasped and whirled, her hand to her mouth. In the gleam from a streetlight, I saw wide eyes and a close-fitting cap of blond hair. She stood staring at me, frozen.

Slowly the woman lowered her hand. It went to her pocket, and I tensed, thinking she might have a gun. All she did, however, was slip her fingers in there. Her other hand clutched the strap of her shoulder bag.

At that moment the entry lights, which were probably on a timer switch, came on. They showed a woman about forty, too sharp-featured to be attractive. Lines of strain were drawn taut around her mouth. She glanced from side to side, as if surprised to find herself there. Her obvious fright relieved me.

She ran her tongue over her lips. "I . . ."

"Look," I said, "I'm not going to hurt you. I just want to know why you're following me."

"I . . . I saw you come out of Abe Snelling's house."

"Yes?"

"So I followed you."

"Do you make a habit of following all his visitors?"

"I . . . no, of course not." She took her hand out of her pocket and placed it on the other one, gripping the shoulder bag even tighter.

"Then why me?"

"I thought you might have been there to see Jane."

"Jane Anthony?"

She nodded.

"What about Jane?"

"She's a friend of mine. I haven't been able to get hold of her. She missed a lunch date early this week, and I've called and called, but Snelling just says she's not there."

"But why watch the house?"

"Tonight was the first time I've done anything like that. I was thinking of going in to talk to Abe Snelling when I saw you come out." She looked down. "I'm afraid."

"Of what?"

She was silent.

"What's your name?" I asked.

"Schaff. Liz Schaff."

It wasn't one of the names on the list of Jane's friends Snelling had given me. "Okay, Liz, mine's Sharon McCone. What exactly are you afraid of?"

"I. . ." She looked up. "Can we go some place and talk?"

"Sure." I didn't want to take this stranger into my apartment, so I said, "Let's go over to Ellen T's, the bar on the corner. We'll have a drink and you can tell me about it."

She nodded and we went down the steps and across Guerrero to my neighborhood tavern.

It was Monday night and the drinking crowd was sparse, just a few regulars. I waved to one of my fellow tenants, a guy who did wood sculpture, and nodded to the owner of the new ice cream shop on the opposite corner. The shop was the latest in an invasion of chic businesses that threatened to change the simple, friendly atmosphere of my working-class neighborhood. Ellen T's was one institution I hoped would remain the same—and I was reasonably certain that as long as Ellen and Stanley Tortelli owned it, it would stay a homey corner tavern, dispensing good food, good drinks, and, occasionally, good advice.

I asked Liz Schaff what she wanted to drink and, when Stanley looked up from one of his ever-present crossword puzzles, ordered two glasses of white wine.

"Red's better for you, now that the fall weather's setting in," Stanley said. Often the good advice came unasked for.

"White," I said firmly.

He shrugged and went to pour it. When I paid, Liz tried to give me a dollar, but I pushed it aside. "Don't worry; I'm on an expense account."

Stanley rolled his eyes at the ceiling. Clearly, he didn't

believe it. As I led Liz to the back room where the old men played dominoes, I wondered why it was that those who knew me well refused to associate me with such items as expense accounts, first-class airplane tickets, and fashionable clothes. Looking down at my jeans and old suede jacket, I got my answer.

The back room was also Monday-night quiet. Four old men sat at the domino tables and two Latino youths were idly knocking balls around on the felt of a pool table. Liz and I sat in the far corner. I sipped my wine before I spoke.

"Now," I said, "tell me what you're afraid of that makes you watch Abe Snelling's house."

Liz ran a hand through her smooth blond hair, then began fiddling with one of her gold hoop earrings. "Well, Jane's missing."

But that wasn't enough. "And?"

"And . . ." She paused, looking at me, and then her eyes took on a hard resolve. "And I'm afraid Abe Snelling has done something to her."

"Done something? Like what?"

"Well, hurt her or imprisoned her in there or . . ."

"Yes?"

"Or killed her."

"Killed her? Do you know Snelling personally?"

She looked startled. "Uh, no."

"He's a photographer, very well known and respected."

"All Jane ever told me was his name. And I don't know anything at all about photography."

"Well, believe me, your suspicions don't jibe with his

public persona. Exactly why do you think he would kill your friend?"

"She's missing. *Something's* happened to her."

"It could be something quite harmless. She may have gotten sick of everything and taken off some place to be alone. She might be with a friend—a male friend. She may have simply decided to disappear; people deliberately disappear all the time."

"Not Jane."

"You never know what a person is capable of doing until he or she does it."

Liz shook her close-cropped head.

"You say you and Jane are friends?" I asked.

She ignored the question. "Snelling must have mentioned Jane to you. What did he say?"

I hesitated. Snelling hadn't asked me to keep the investigation confidential. "That she's missing."

"Are you a friend of his? Is that why he told you?"

"I'm a private detective. Snelling hired me to find her."

"Oh." Liz reached for her wineglass. Her hand shook slightly as she raised it to her lips. She set it back down carefully in the indentation it had made on her napkin. The gesture made me think of Jane Anthony's immaculate bedroom. "He must also be worried about her then."

"Very worried. So you see, your fears are groundless. Murderers don't hire private detectives to locate their victims, now do they?"

She smiled faintly. "Not in real life."

"That's right." I sipped some wine. "If you want to

help me find your friend, you can tell me something about her."

"Like what?"

"Start at the beginning—how do you know her?"

"We're from the same hometown, Salmon Bay, near Port San Marco. I'm about four years older than Jane, but we knew each other growing up—everybody in Salmon Bay knows everybody else. And we worked together at The Tidepools."

"What's that?"

"A hospice, a place that provides care for the terminally ill. I'm a registered nurse, have my degree from UCLA. Jane is a social worker."

"Where is The Tidepools?"

"In Salmon Bay, a little north of the village proper. It's a rambling shingled building on the bluff above a beach with reefs and tidepools. The setting is beautiful, really, all cypress and eucalyptus groves. You'd never think, looking at it, that people go there to die."

"And you and Jane worked there together."

"For over five years."

"It must have been depressing."

Liz looked surprised. "Oh, no, it wasn't. The whole philosophy of the hospice movement is dying without fear, and in dignity. At The Tidepools, the patients live out what time they have fully, even happily. Sometimes it can be quite inspiring."

"When did you leave there?"

"Well over a year ago. There was . . . some . . . unpleasantness, and then I had a good offer from S.F. General."

"Unpleasantness?"

She shook her head and looked down into her wine.

I let it go for the moment. "What about Jane? Did she leave at the same time?"

"No, not until maybe eight months ago. She came up here without a job, hoping she'd find something in her field, but she found that they're not hiring social workers. She had it pretty rough until Abe Snelling took her in. I tried to make her a loan but Jane's too proud to accept money."

But not too proud to accept Snelling's free room, I thought. "Do you know of any place Jane might have gone?" I asked. "Friends? A boyfriend?"

"No." She looked up, eyes wide. "That's why I've been so worried."

"What about home? I understand her mother still lives in Salmon Bay."

"They don't get along. I don't think she'd go there."

Briefly I'd entertained the thought that maybe Jane didn't want to see Snelling for some reason and had asked her mother to lie to him on the phone. But if they weren't on good terms... "You're sure it's that bad a relationship?"

Liz hesitated. "Pretty sure. Mrs. Anthony doesn't approve of anything Jane does."

"Why?"

"That's just the way she is."

"I don't understand."

"Salmon Bay is a rather provincial place. It's basically a fishing village, but the fishing industry got automated and most of the individual fisheries went broke. People in

Salmon Bay still manage to make a living, but barely. They just sit out there on their spit of land, mending their nets and dreaming of the good old days. Naturally, anyone who ventures into the real world is suspect.'' The bitterness in Liz's voice grew with every word.

''By 'anyone,' you mean Jane.''

''Yes.'' She drained her wineglass. ''Jane. And me.''

Liz Schaff hadn't given me any more concrete facts than Snelling, but her short, resentful speech about Salmon Bay had breathed life into the photograph I had in my bag. I finished my wine and slipped into my jacket.

''Have I helped?'' Liz asked.

''Yes. Thank you.''

''Will you let me know what you find out?''

''Sure.'' I gave her one of my cards. ''The first number is where I work—All Souls Legal Cooperative; the other's my answering service. Call me anytime if you think of anything else.''

Liz scribbled a number on the back of what looked like a grocery list. ''And that's where you can reach me. Please do let me know.''

I told her not to worry, and we left together. Liz headed for her car and I went home to pack for a trip to Salmon Bay.

3

I couldn't decide whether my studio apartment was untidy or just looked that way in contrast to Jane Anthony's impeccable room. True, there were unwashed dishes in the sink and rumpled quilts on the bed, but that didn't necessarily make me a sloven, did it? As I entered the combination living-and-bedroom, my cat, Watney, brushed against my legs, purring as if to reassure me. I scratched him and then sat down cross-legged on the bed, staring at the want ad section that was spread out there.

The ads from the Sunday paper were turned to the heading "APARTMENTS FOR RENT—S.F.," and a good number of the boxes were circled in red ink. Unfortunately, most of them had X's over the circles. When I'd decided it was time to start looking for a new place to live, I hadn't realized what a short supply of decent apartments there was in the city.

But I'd definitely decided to move. There had been two murders in the building the previous year—which I had been involved with—as well as numerous upheavals in the neighborhood stemming from the crimes. Frankly, coming home depressed me these days. And the apartment really was too small; the sparklies in the acoustical paint on the ceiling were tacky; the old icebox that ran off the compressor in the basement didn't hold enough or keep things very cold; even the little garden of plastic flowers in the lobby had ceased to amuse me. It was time to move.

Wasn't it?

But I'd been here for years. I was settled.

Wasn't I?

Besides, was I really ready to pay over six hundred dollars for a one-bedroom in another neighborhood?

I cut the debate with myself short. Obviously I wasn't going any place in a hurry; all the apartments I'd looked at yesterday had been rented by the time I'd gotten there.

I reached for the phone and called my answering service. There was a message from my friend Linnea Carraway, who had recently taken a news anchor position with a small TV station in Seattle; she'd just called to chat. Paula Mercer, my artistic friend from the de Young Museum, had heard of an apartment I might like and wanted me to phone her. One of my sisters had called. All she'd said to the operator at the service was, "This is Sharon's sister," so I didn't know which of the two she was. And I was damned if I was going to spend long-distance money to find out. There was no message from Greg.

Well, why should there be? That was over. After a year and a half, Lieutenant Gregory Marcus and I had called it off. We'd had good times—even wonderful times—but our stormy natures had turned our affair into a battleground. I was glad the relationship was over; it was a relief to be without the constant, energy-sapping conflict. But still, you get used to that daily phone call after all that time. You get used to shared laughter and loving and nice moments. Not finding a message left me with a mild sense of depression. I needed to do something. I needed to get out of here. Now.

I got up and took my suitcase from the closet. Watney eyed it suspiciously.

"Yes, I'm leaving you again," I told him. "Tim will feed you."

Watney merely turned his back and licked one black-and-white spotted shoulder.

That was another problem, I thought as I threw jeans and sweaters, and a skirt in case I needed to look grown up, into the bag. Where would I ever find another apartment manager who would take such good care of my cat? Maybe I should . . .

"Enough, Sharon!" I said aloud. "You've got a case to work on. Let the housing problem take care of itself."

As I drove down the Junipero Serra freeway toward San Jose, I decided to bypass Salmon Bay and take a motel room in Port San Marco. I remembered spending a week there one childhood summer with Linnea and her parents. The memory conjured up images of a boardwalk and amusement park rides, cotton candy and corn dogs.

And the thought of corn dogs made me realize it had been a long time since supper. I fished in my bag for one of my emergency-ration Hershey bars and unwrapped it with one hand. The squares of chocolate lifted those traces of depression that remained.

Port San Marco, as I recalled, had once been a great fishing port. Then, as Liz Schaff had said, the industry had become automated and large companies from the north and south had taken over, putting the individual fisheries out of business. Unlike the village of Salmon Bay, the larger town had made the transition to the modern age, and now so-called smogless industries and expensive housing tracts dotted the hills west of the port. The port itself was given over to tourism; luxurious marinas, restaurants, and hotels lined the waterfront. I'd even heard something about plans for a performing arts center on the site of the old amusement park.

I had liked the town I remembered from my childhood, with its roller coaster and pinball parlors, hot dog stands and beer halls. I would have loved the rough-and-tumble fishing port of yesteryear, but I was quite certain I would not like the shiny new Port San Marco at all. Still, I resolved to get a motel on the waterfront and perhaps recapture some of the holiday feeling of that youthful summer. After all, Snelling was paying my expenses, and he could afford it.

The freeway skirted San Jose and connected with Route 101. To either side were apartment complexes and housing developments, new and insubstantial. These suburbs always reminded me of the sprawl of Los Angeles, and I was glad when I came to the open countryside, with its rolling, oak-dotted hills.

I slipped into a relaxed driving mood and let my mind wander back to my conversation with Liz Schaff. Much as her concern for her friend seemed genuine, I couldn't quite believe her exaggerated fears. The thought of Abe Snelling killing anyone was ridiculous. But, then, Liz had said she didn't know the photographer.

But maybe she did. What kind of a friend doesn't have you to her house at least once in six months? Maybe there had been a meeting between Liz and Abe. Maybe there had been some sort of disagreement that led her to dislike and suspect him. Otherwise, why wouldn't she just come right out and ask about Jane on the phone? Or march up to the front door and demand to know her friend's whereabouts?

I'd have to ask Snelling about Liz Schaff.

The drive south was going quickly. Salinas was already behind me, and I was high on the ridge heading for Paso Robles and the Port San Marco cutoff. I debated another Hershey bar, but decided I'd be there in time to check into a motel and have a snack before everything closed down for the night.

All right, I thought, Jane and Liz were friends in Salmon Bay. The little village sounded closed off, perhaps hostile. At the very least I'd encounter coldness there. And, if Jane's relations with her mother were really as bad as Liz claimed, I might have difficulty getting information from her. Label Salmon Bay a possible trouble spot.

And what about this hospice called The Tidepools?

What had Liz said? Something about some unpleasantness. And then she'd refused to elaborate. Had she been fired? No, she'd said she'd had an offer from S.F. General. Maybe Jane had been fired. Maybe that was the reason she'd had such trouble finding work in San Francisco. I'd check with the personnel office at The Tidepools. . . .

Caught up in my plans, I almost missed the Port San Marco turnoff. The road climbed into the dark hills, then descended in a sweeping curve. Ahead of me I spotted the black expanse of the sea. Port San Marco formed a crescent of light along the shore. I followed the main road through town to the boulevard that ran along the beachfront.

The Mission Inn across from the wharf appealed to me. It was Spanish-style stucco, two stories, with an interior courtyard full of palm trees and bougainvillea. A turquoise swimming pool gleamed coldly in the darkness. I registered and was given an upstairs corner room with a view of the harbor. After nodding approvingly at the king-size bed and automatic coffee maker, I called All Souls and left my number, then set out for the wharf in search of food.

Here, at least, the town hadn't changed. The wharf was still lined with charter fishing boats, souvenir shops, and restaurants. I chose the one at the very end, an unpretentious place with booths and a shell-and-fishnet motif. When the waitress brought my crab sandwich, I asked her how far it was to Salmon Bay.

"About ten miles up the shoreline highway. I don't know why you'd want to go there, though."

"Why not? What's it like?"

"Like nothing. A bunch of tumbledown houses. A few beer-and-bait shacks."

"People up there still fish for a living?"

"If you can call it a living."

"What about a place called The Tidepools? Do you know anything about that?"

She rested one hip against the table of the opposite booth, obviously welcoming a long conversation. She was in her fifties and, even in the subdued light of the restaurant, looked tired. "Yeah. It's a pretty fancy place, like a nursing home, only they don't let you in there unless you're dying."

"Is it expensive?"

"I guess it would be. There was an article in the paper about it once. Says they have a new way of dealing with death there." She shrugged. "I don't know. Seems to me there's only one way to deal with it—and that's to go through it."

"I guess."

She shifted from one foot to the other, a thoughtful look on her face. "You know, I get the feeling they're playing games up there."

"Games?"

"You know, trying to pretend they're really not going to die. Playing games to keep the dark away."

The phrase sent a shiver up my spine. "Aren't we all?"

"Yeah, aren't we?" She straightened, glancing over at the cash register where a dark-haired man was counting change. "I better get back to work. You want something to drink with that? Some wine?"

"Sure. White."

I ate my crab sandwich and drank my wine, and afterward I had a second glass, staring out at the water and the people who passed on the wharf. It was not the height of the season, but the tourists were in good supply. They strolled hand-in-hand or walked together, yet apart. I imagined that for some couples the vacation had brought them closer; for others, it had only reminded them of their loneliness.

I thought about Greg and me and wondered how it would have been for us. We'd never had the chance to find out, and now we never would. Sometimes I wondered if I'd ever again be one of the ones holding hands and, for a time, banishing loneliness—playing games to keep my own dark away.

4

By morning my private demons had returned to whichever corner of my mind they usually resided in—for a long stay, I hoped. I got up, turned the coffee maker on, took a shower, and then called Jane Anthony's mother. She was reluctant to talk to any friend of Jane's at first, but finally agreed to see me at eleven, after she did her marketing. I had eggs and bacon in the motel coffee shop and then set out for Salmon Bay.

It was a warm day with only the slightest hint of fall in the air, and what fog there was promised to burn off quickly. I followed the Shoreline Highway north, past an expansive housing development with a golf course, into farmland. Pumpkin fields, colorful with their ripe fruit, stretched west toward the sea; to the east were the sunbrowned hills. After eight or nine miles, the land curved, forming a little bay where boats rode at anchor. Half a mile farther a left-turn lane with a flashing amber light and a weathered sign indicated the road to Salmon Bay.

It was actually more of a lane, rough and not recently paved. I put the car in low gear and bumped across a field covered with scrub vegetation. The pavement meandered for a while and then paralleled the shore. The first thing I came to was a boatyard surrounded by a chain link fence. Full of no-nonsense fishing craft upon hoists for repairs, it seemed deserted save for one man who was scraping paint from the bow of an old green boat. I continued on, past Johnson's Marine Supply, Rose's Crab Shack, and a general store. Soon unpaved lanes lined with ramshackle houses began appearing to my right. None of them had street signs.

I hadn't asked Mrs. Anthony for directions to her house. Who would have thought it necessary in a village the size of Salmon Bay? I kept going, passing the Shorebird Bar and a place advertising bait, and finally ended up at a dilapidated pier that looked like nobody had set foot on it in years. Two brown-and-white mongrels trotted along the side of the road, but otherwise I saw no one. All the businesses except for the general store were closed.

I turned the MG in front of the pier and went all the way back to the boatyard. No, there wasn't a single street sign in town. After parking near the gap in the chain link fence, I got out of the car and went into the yard. The shack that served as an office was also closed, and the only sounds were the cries of seagulls and the steady scraping of the man's putty knife on the boat. I started toward him, glancing at the craft at anchor.

These were not the luxurious pleasure boats of the Port San Marco marinas, but clumsy utilitarian vessels that had seen better days. A wharf with fuel pumps ran along the edge of the water, but there was no one to man them and no customers either. Had it not been for the man working on the boat, I would have felt I'd stepped into a long-abandoned stage set for a seafaring drama. My feet crunched on the gravel as I approached him, but the man did not look around.

"Excuse me," I said.

He glared at me, nodded curtly, and went on with his scraping. He had black hair, a full beard, and, although he couldn't have been much more than forty, a face as tanned and leathery as an old man's.

"I'm looking for Hydrangea Lane. Can you—"

"Who are you looking for?"

"I'm sorry?"

"Who on Hydrangea Lane?"

"A Mrs. Anthony. Sylvia Anthony."

The putty knife faltered in its regular motion. "She know you're coming?"

"Yes, she does."

He stopped his work and wiped the putty knife on his faded jeans. "You sure?"

I'd expected coldness, but not the third degree. "Of course I'm sure. Look—"

"Just asking." His tone was mild, but his dark eyes were narrowed in suspicion.

"Well, can you tell me how to get there? I didn't see any street signs."

"Of course not." His lips turned up in a mirthless smile. "There aren't any."

"How does anyone find anybody else?"

"Don't need street signs to do that."

"Maybe not if you live here, but what about outsiders?"

The smile dropped off his face. "We don't welcome outsiders here." There was ill-concealed menace in the words and his hand seemed to tighten on the putty knife.

I stood my ground. "I guess you don't. But Mrs. Anthony is expecting me, and I don't want to keep her waiting."

The man regarded me for a moment, then turned back to the boat and began scraping again. "You go along to the last lane on the right. Take it to the end, then turn left. It's a white house with a driftwood fence and blue hydrangeas, lots of them. That's where you'll find her."

I thanked him and got out of there, vaguely oppressed by his senseless hostility. Were all the residents of the village like that? I wondered. Or had I stumbled across the one hardened case?

Thc boatyard man had meant it about lots of hydrangeas. They filled Mrs. Anthony's tiny front yard, their blue blossoms escaping through the misshapen crossbars of the driftwood fence and cascading onto the front porch. The house was freshly painted, in contrast to its neighbors, which were shabby and, in a couple of cases, surrounded by junk-filled yards. I went through the gate and along a shell-bordered walk, and knocked at the door. The shades on the windows were pulled to the sills and for a moment I wondered if Jane's mother had returned from her marketing trip.

In a few seconds, however, the door opened and a tall, gaunt woman looked out at me. She was the woman in Snelling's photo grown older, with gray hair instead of black and wrinkles where Jane's flesh was smooth. Deep lines bracketed her mouth from her prominent nose to her chin. Briefly I wondered if Jane would look like this in twenty or thirty years, or if getting out of Salmon Bay had put her beyond the reach of the bitterness that had so aged her mother.

I introduced myself and Mrs. Anthony ushered me into a dark parlor. It was crammed with what looked like good antiques—a rolltop desk among them—and every surface was covered with china knicknacks. My first impression was of clutter, but as my eyes became accustomed to the dimness, I saw that each object was carefully placed and dust free. Jane was her mother's girl in more than looks.

Mrs. Anthony indicated I should sit on the couch and lowered herself slowly into a platform rocker, the way a person afflicted with arthritis will do. She snapped on a floorlamp next to her and I looked for signs of the poor health Snelling had mentioned. There weren't any, but many illnesses are hard to spot; broaching the subject of Jane's disappearance would still require care and tact.

Before I could speak, Mrs. Anthony said, "You mentioned on the telephone that you're a friend of my daughter's. What brings you to Salmon Bay?"

"I'm trying to locate Jane."

"Why?"

"I need to talk to her."

"About what?"

I decided to ignore the question. "Do you know where Jane is, Mrs. Anthony?"

An odd look passed over her face. It could have been anger or perhaps fear. Whatever, it was gone before I could put a label on it. "No."

"Have you seen her recently?"

She was silent a moment. "What if I have?"

"Mrs. Anthony, I really need to locate Jane. It would help me tremendously if—"

"Why should I help you?"

"You would also be helping your daughter. It's very important I talk to her."

"About what?"

"I'm afraid I can't say."

She hesitated. I sensed she was unsure which would be in her daughter's best interest—protecting her privacy or putting me in touch with her. "It's very important, you say?"

"Yes."

"All right; she was here last night."

"Last night?"

"Yes, came to pay her old mother a visit." She spoke the words with a biting sarcasm.

"How long did she stay?"

"An hour, maybe less. That's about the usual length of one of her visits."

"Did you tell her her friend Abe Snelling had been trying to get in touch with her?"

She raised her eyebrows. "And what do you know of Abe Snelling?"

"We're both her friends—"

"Seems Jane has a lot of friends all of a sudden. Funny, for a girl who never did." She got up and went to raise one of the window shades, as if to throw light on the subject of her friendless daughter. Turning, she said, "Look, Miss McCone, I told Jane that Abe Snelling had called. She said she'd get back to him when she could. And then she left."

"And she didn't say where she was going?"

Again the odd expression crossed her face. This time I put a name to it: disgust. "No. My daughter does not confide in me."

I thought she was going to ask me to leave, but instead she returned to the rocker and settled in. It occurred to me that she was lonely and glad she had someone to talk to. I glanced around the room, trying to find a way to keep the conversation going, and spotted a framed photograph. It was of the old pier I'd seen before, moody and mysterious in the fog. I got up and went to look closer.

"That's a nice picture," I said.

"Jane took it."

"I didn't know she was a photographer." But as I spoke I realized Snelling had said they had a mutual interest in art.

"She isn't anymore. She doesn't do anything but live off—" Abruptly she cut off her own words.

"You mean live off Abe Snelling? He's only helping her out until she finds a social work job."

Mrs. Anthony sighed. "Him too?"

"What?"

"Nothing. A social work job, eh? I warned her about choosing work like that. You depend too much on the government, and the government isn't to be trusted. Now she's out of a livelihood, just like her father was when the fishing went bust."

"Jane's father was a fisherman?"

"All his life. Didn't know anything else. When the fishing went bust, he didn't know what to do with himself. He's dead now; been dead nearly thirty years." Her voice had taken on a bitter singsong quality, as if this were a speech she'd repeated many times in those thirty years. "I raised my girl all by myself, working as a maid for the so-called fine folks in Port San Marco. I saw she had everything, just like the other kids. And she repaid me. How she repaid me!" She laughed hollowly.

I stood very still, not wanting to break the train of her memories. "How?" I said softly.

"I had the money saved. I was going to send her to art school in Port San Marco so she could maybe make something of her photography. She could have lived at home, helped out with a part-time job. But, no, not for her. She had to go away to college, up to San Jose. And she had to get fancy ideas about what she called social responsibility, working with those less fortunate than her. Those were her exact words—'those less fortunate than I am.' If she wanted to help someone less fortunate, she only had to look to her own mother."

She fell silent and I moved back to the sofa. "When did Jane come back from San Jose?"

"After about a year of working with bums and drug

addicts. I thought she was cured of that 'social responsibility' nonsense. But, no, she had to go and get a job at The Tidepools, working with more 'unfortunates.' Unfortunates, my hat!"

"Why do you say that?"

"You have to be rich to get in there. Rich and dying. But do they pay their help well? No, they don't. Jane had to moonlight, working at a drug abuse clinic in her off time. And she wasn't the only one. Her friend Liz did too—at the Safeco Pharmacy. And what did Jane spend that extra money on? Did she come home and help out? No, she moved to a fancy apartment in Port San Marco and took up with that Don. Oh, Don was all right; I know that now. She's done far worse in her time . . ." Her voice ran down and she stared into space, probably cataloging all the men who had been worse than Don.

"Mrs. Anthony," I said, "what's Don's last name?"

She shook her head. "We'll leave him out of this."

"She may have gone to see him—"

"No, not Don. He wouldn't have her. Not after what she did."

"What did she—"

"No." She shook her head firmly. "That's over. I won't go into it."

I sighed. "So you have no idea where she's gone now?"

"I don't know, and I don't care." But her eyes said she did care. "The reason you need to see her—is it about a job?"

I hated to disappoint her. "No. Actually, Mrs. Anthony, I don't know your daughter."

Her sad eyes became puzzled. "But you said—"

"I'm a private detective; Abe Snelling hired me to find Jane. She left home a week ago without telling him where she was going, and Abe was afraid something had happened to her."

"A private detective." She shook her head slowly. "The kinds of jobs you girls will get into today. . . . This Abe Snelling—is he in love with Jane?"

"They're just friends, but good friends."

"That's good. She never had many friends, you know. She never fit in here in the village. The other children thought she was different . . . and I guess they were right. I'm glad she has a friend like Abe Snelling."

"So am I, Mrs. Anthony." I stood up.

Mrs. Anthony stood up too. "You must think I'm a bad mother, Miss McCone."

"Not really."

"You must understand—I love my daughter."

"I'm sure you do."

"If I didn't love her, she wouldn't be able to make me so angry."

"Of course. I understand."

She looked into my eyes, her hand on the front doorknob. "Do you have children, Miss McCone?"

"No, I don't."

"Then you can't understand."

"Yes, I can. I also have a mother."

As I went down the front walk, Mrs. Anthony lowered the shade on the window once again. It reminded me of Abe Snelling locking himself inside his house with his treasured solitude.

5

I went back to the motel and called Snelling to report what I'd found out. "So," I concluded, "it appears Jane is all right and will get in touch with you when the spirit moves her."

There was a pause. "Well, so far she hasn't. And her mother gave her my message last night."

"I guess she doesn't think it that urgent."

"No, I guess not." He hesitated again. "Sharon, she's got to be staying somewhere in the Port San Marco area. Since you're already down there, would you keep looking for her?"

"I can, but it seems a lot of expense for nothing."

"I'd appreciate it if you would, though. Don't worry about the expense. Just find Jane—I must speak to her."

Snelling obviously had more reason for wanting to talk to Jane than merely reassuring himself she was all right. What? Well, that wasn't really any of my business and, if he was willing to pay for my time, I didn't mind pursuing his elusive roommate. In fact, I was enjoying being out of the city. "Okay," I said, "I'll keep looking." Then I remembered the man named Don. "Abe, did Jane ever mention someone named Don, an old boyfriend?"

"Don? No, the name doesn't ring a bell."

"Terrific. There must be hundreds of Dons in the area."

"Do you think Jane's with him?"

"Her mother says no, but it's a possibility."

"Why can't you ask Mrs. Anthony who he is?"

"I did; she wouldn't say."

His sigh was audible over the wire. "Mothers . . ."

Then I thought of someone who probably would know—and tell. "Abe, do you know a friend of Jane's called Liz Schaff?"

He was silent for a moment. "Liz who?"

"Schaff. S-c-h-a-f-f."

"I don't recall her."

So Liz had been telling the truth about not knowing Snelling. Odd that Jane had never had Liz over to the house. But then, her mother had indicated that Jane didn't make friends easily; maybe once she had one she didn't treat her the way most people do.

"Who is this Liz person?" Snelling asked.

"A nurse at S.F. General. She and Jane had a lunch appointment and Jane never showed. Liz was worried about her."

"How do you know her?"

"I can't go into that now." I looked at my watch.

"Listen, Abe, I'm going to check a few things out and then I'll be in touch, probably this evening."

"Okay." He seemed reluctant to hang up. "Keep me posted."

I placed a second call to San Francisco, to the number Liz Schaff had scribbled on the back of her grocery list. She answered on the third ring.

"It's funny you got hold of me," she said when I identified myself. "Usually I'm at work, the noon-to-eight shift, but I'm off sick today."

"I hope it's nothing serious."

"Just a cold. Have you found Jane?"

"She's somewhere in the Port San Marco area; at least, she visited her mother last night."

"Then she's okay."

"I guess so. Her mother would have noticed if anything was wrong."

"Don't count on it. What did you think of Salmon Bay?"

"Not much." Everyone was certainly talkative today. "Liz, I've got a question for you. Do you know a former boyfriend of Jane's named Don?"

"Sure, that would be Don Del Boccio. He's a disc jockey in Port San Marco, on KPSM."

"Do you think she might have gone to see him?"

"I doubt it. Not after..."

"After what?"

"Well, they broke up quite a while ago."

"Mrs. Anthony didn't want to talk about it. She hinted Jane had done something bad to him."

Liz chuckled. "Probably did. Jane is not exactly easy on her men."

"Well, I think I'll talk to him anyway. Thanks for the information." I hung up before she could further prolong the conversation.

In the motel office I bought a local paper, then walked out on the wharf to the restaurant where I'd eaten the night before. While I was waiting for my shrimp salad, I scanned the radio listings. The show called "Don's Daily Doubles" was on from two to eight; they worked their disc jockeys hard here. Since it was almost two now, I decided to save Del Boccio for evening and check out The Tidepools this afternoon on the off chance that Jane had visited her former place of employment. When I got in my car, I tuned in KPSM.

Del Boccio's voice came on, extolling the Golden Forty Hits. He intended to play them all, over and over, two at a time without commercial interruptions, for the next six hours. He had a frantic style that matched the station's hard rock format—and made me cringe. After a few minutes I switched the radio off. It was enough to know he was on the air and unavailable until eight; I didn't have to listen to him. And, while Del Boccio was honking, snorting, and screeching his way into the hearts of local teenagers, I might even catch up with Jane. Then I wouldn't have to deal with him at all.

The Tidepools was as attractive as Liz Schaff had said. A low building of weathered gray shingles, it was laid out in several wings on a bluff overlooking the Pacific. There were great expanses of glass that must have afforded magnificent views of the surf crashing on the rugged reefs below. Groves of eucalyptus and wind-bent cypress were scattered throughout the grounds, and the rolling lawn was immaculate. I parked in a semicircular driveway and went up to the front wing, the windows of which were screened by tall juniper hedges.

I pushed through the heavy carved door into a Spanish-style lobby with a gleaming terra-cotta floor. The rear wall was all glass and opened onto a courtyard with a blue mosaic fountain and fuchsia plants in hanging baskets. The woman at the desk matched the decor: she was as darkly handsome as an Indian maiden brought into a *hacienda* to wait on the *rancheros*.

I gave her my card and asked to see the personnel director. She dialed her phone and had a muffled conversation, then replaced the receiver and looked up at me. "Mrs. Bates is in conference right now. Perhaps you'd like to walk around the grounds while you wait? It shouldn't be more than fifteen minutes."

A walk appealed to me far more than sitting on one of the hard carved-wood chairs in the reception area. I went back outside and looked around. Eucalyptus bordered the semicircular drive on either side, and farther back, toward the edge of the bluff, clumps of cypress leaned to indicate the direction of the prevailing wind. I cut across the well-manicured lawn toward the cliff. A wooden platform with wicker chairs perched there, and a pair of white-haired ladies sat together, knitting and chatting. They didn't look ill, and they certainly didn't seem sad or afraid. In fact, they nodded pleasantly at me and went on with their conversation.

I looked down at the sea. Huge outcroppings of black rock rose from the placid water, up and down the sheltered beach. A long stairway scaled the side of the cliff from the platform. I climbed down it, noting the high tide line of seaweed and shells. When the tide was in, the entire beach would be submerged. The reefs, with the exception of one or two huge ones, would disappear—and the waves crashing against them would be treacherous. I took off my boots and socks and walked across the damp sand to the water's edge. When I tested it with my toes, it was as cold as I'd expected.

But so what? Born in San Diego, I'd grown up around the sea. To me, walking on a beach without getting my feet wet was practically heresy and, besides, I wanted to get a look at the tidepools for which the hospice was named. I rolled up my pants legs and waded out to the start of the reefs.

The rocks felt rough even on my feet, which were toughened by my habit of going barefoot whenever possible. I squatted down and peered into one of the pools formed by concavities in the reef. Tiny fish darted through the trapped waters, and starfish and anemones clung to the sides, their delicate arms drawn in and still. Tidepools—microcosms of the unfathomable sea—had always fascinated me. I watched this one for several minutes, until I realized it was time for my appointment with Mrs. Bates.

The white-haired ladies were gone when I reached the platform. I sat down on a wicker chair and brushed sand from my feet before putting on my socks and boots. Then I recrossed the lawn and entered the main building. The receptionist picked up her phone when she saw me and, minutes later, a slender woman with sleekly styled gray hair entered through an archway. She was dressed in a tailored black suit that would have looked more at home on Montgomery Street than in this coastal setting, and the smooth lines of her face indicated the gray was premature.

"Ms. McCone? I'm Ann Bates, the personnel director here." She extended her hand.

I clasped it briefly. "Thank you for taking the time to see me."

"I understand you're a private detective." She glanced at my card, which she held in her other hand.

"Yes. I'm investigating the disappearance of one of your former employees."

She raised one finely penciled eyebrow. "Who might that be?"

"Jane Anthony. I believe she was a social worker here up until eight months ago."

Ann Bates frowned. "Yes, she was. But why have you come to us now?"

"Apparently Jane is somewhere in the Port San Marco area. I thought she might have come to see you, perhaps in hopes of getting her old job back. She hasn't found work since she left your employ."

"I haven't seen Jane since the day she terminated." She spoke abruptly, and her choice of words made it sound as if Jane were dead.

"Well, you knew her, at any rate. Maybe you can tell me something that would shed some light on where she might be."

"I doubt anything I have to say would be helpful."

"Another of your former employees, Liz Schaff, mentioned some unpleasantness that occurred here before they both quit. Did it involve Jane?"

Ann Bates glanced over her shoulder at the receptionist, who had been listening to our conversation. The woman quickly dropped her eyes to a book on the desk. "I don't know what she meant by 'unpleasantness,'" Mrs. Bates said.

"Neither do I, but she definitely alluded to it. Can you think—"

"Ms. McCone, I have no idea what Ms. Schaff could have been thinking of. And, frankly, I'm going to have to cut this short. I can't help you, and it's against The Tidepools' policy to discuss our employees—or former employees—with anyone."

"Surely you can make an exception in this case. Jane's been missing for a week."

"I thought you said she was here in the area. How can she be missing if you know where she is?"

"I only know approximately where. Please—"

"At any rate, it's not in my power to make exceptions to our rule."

"Who can, then?"

She looked puzzled.

"You must have a supervisor."

"The only person here with more authority than I is our director, Dr. Allen Keller."

"Then let me talk to him."

"He's not available today."

"When will he be?"

She made an impatient gesture with one hand and glanced at the receptionist, who still had her head bowed over the book. "Dr. Keller is taking the week off."

"Is he at home?"

"He may be."

"Then let me call him there. This is important."

"To you, perhaps, but not to Dr. Keller. His telephone number is unlisted, and I cannot give it out to anyone."

"Shouldn't Dr. Keller be the one to judge what's important to him?"

Her face reddened. "In this instance, I am sure I can speak for him." She stepped around me to the door and held it open. "And now, Ms. McCone, I must ask you to leave."

"Thanks for being so helpful." Irritated, I stalked outside. The door slammed behind me.

"Officious bitch," I said aloud. There was no one to hear me but a seagull on the lawn. I glared at it and went to my car. Allen Keller might have an unlisted phone number, I thought, but there were ways to get his address.

6

Back in my motel room, I thumbed through the Yellow Pages and selected a few of the more exclusive-sounding men's clothing stores. Apparently Allen Keller didn't shop at the first two I called, but the credit clerk at the third reacted with dismay when I identified myself as Dr. Keller's secretary and asked why he hadn't received his most recent monthly statement.

She went to check her files and returned to the phone a few minutes later. "That statement went out on the twenty-eighth, ma'am."

"That's odd. Was it sent to the Beach Walk address?" Beach Walk was one of the few residential street names in Port San Marco that I remembered.

"No, it went to Sea View Drive."

"Ninety-six Sea View?"

"No, seventy-seven."

"Now I understand." I scribbled down the address and

added, not without a twinge of conscience, "That should have been changed. It's ninety-six Beach Walk now. You'll see it's corrected?"

"Of course, ma'am." Relief flooded her voice; I wasn't going to yell at her.

I wasn't familiar enough with Port San Marco to place Sea View Drive. A map on the wall of the motel office showed it to be in a new development southeast of downtown. I picked out what looked like the easiest route and set off to talk to Dr. Keller.

The development was a maze of newly paved streets spiraling up toward the tops of the oak-dotted hills. I followed Sea View Drive higher and higher until I had a view of the entire coast and the channel islands in the distance. Keller's house was an arrangement of shingle-and-glass boxes whose roofs slanted at various angles; the shingles had barely had time to weather. The place reminded me of a hastily assembled house of cards that might topple at any moment.

The heavy blond man who answered the door wore a blue terrycloth bathrobe and slippers. He was fortyish and at least thirty pounds overweight. The puffiness of his face and his bloodshot eyes suggested he liked his alcohol as much as his food. "What is it?" he asked impatiently.

"I'm looking for Dr. Allen Keller."

"You've found him."

"My name's Sharon McCone. I'm an investigator with All Souls Legal Cooperative in San Francisco." I held out my card.

He looked at it with distaste. "You're a detective?"

"Yes. I'm trying to locate—"

"Is it about my divorce?"

"No, I'm—"

"Because if it is, you can tell Arlene she's gotten all she's going to get."

"It's not about your divorce."

"I don't care about the community property laws. I made it, and it's mine, and she can—"

I raised my voice. "It's not about your divorce!"

"Oh." Temporarily deflated, Keller surveyed me. "Come to think of it, you don't look like any of the detectives I've seen this past year. And Lord knows I've seen enough of them. Are you sure you're not working for Arlene?"

"I'm sure. I've never even met your wife."

"You're not missing much." He looked thoughtful. "Tell me, can you make a fried egg sandwich?"

"A what?"

"Fried egg sandwich."

"Well, yes, but what has that got to do—"

"Come on." He opened the door wider and motioned me inside.

I hesitated, then shrugged and stepped into a large entryway. Keller shut the door and started for the rear of the house.

"I like them gooey," he said over his shoulder, "but I keep breaking the yolks."

"I like them that way too." I followed him. "There are two kinds of people: the ones who break the yolk before frying the egg and the ones who don't. It's like people who use sandwich spread versus people who use real mayonnaise."

"And Scotch drinkers versus bourbon drinkers. Or people who eat small curd cottage cheese, as opposed to the ones who like large curds." Keller led me into a large, tiled kitchen. It was spotlessly clean except for the stove top, which was littered with egg shells. A partly fried egg with a broken yolk sat in congealing grease in a frying pan. There were several more eggs in the sink. Keller motioned at the stove. "See what you can do. Fix one for yourself if you're hungry."

Never shy where food was concerned, I jumped at the invitation; after all, it was almost five o'clock. "Thanks, I will."

Keller went to the refrigerator. "Want a beer?"

"Sure." I busied myself at the stove.

"The help's off today." He set the beer next to me. "And I can't cook worth a damn. So of course I had to get a craving for something difficult. By the way, since it's not me you're after, what're you investigating?"

"Later. This is a delicate operation."

We took our sandwiches to a blue-and-white breakfast nook. As Keller sat across from me and cracked another beer, I studied him. Under the overhead light, the puffiness of his face was more pronounced and there were bluish semicircles under his eyes. It seemed a typical case of a doctor not taking his own advice. I wondered if he was always in this bad a shape or if it was a result of what sounded like a messy divorce.

After I'd bitten into my sandwich and gotten yolk all over my chin, I dug into my bag and took out Snelling's photo of Jane Anthony. "Do you remember this woman?" I passed it over to Keller.

He looked at it and his eyes widened in surprise. "That's Jane."

"Yes, Jane Anthony."

"Why do you have her picture?"

"She's missing and her roommate has hired me to locate her."

"But . . ." He paused and took a swig of beer.

"But?"

Keller ran a hand through his blond hair. "Why have you come to me?"

"She's a former employee of The Tidepools. Mrs. Bates refused to talk to me about Jane. I thought perhaps you could shed some light on where she might be."

"*I* could?"

"Yes. Her roommate is very anxious to locate her."

"Oh." Keller poked a finger at his untouched sandwich, looking thoughtfully at the picture. "I see. Well, I'd like to help you, but Miss Anthony was merely one of many employees. As an administrator, I don't have much contact with the people who work with the patients, and I'm afraid I don't know anything about the woman personally. And, of course, it's been a long time since I've seen her."

That was what I'd been afraid of. I sighed, taking the photo from him and tucking it back in my bag. Still, while I was here, I could try to find out something about the mysterious "unpleasantness" at The Tidepools. When people refused to talk about something or pretended ignorance of it—and Ann Bates had seemed to be pretending—I became more and more curious.

"Tell me something about The Tidepools, Dr. Keller," I said. "Are you merely the director or do you own it?"

"I'm part owner, along with Mrs. Bates, who is my business manager as well as personnel director." Keller still hadn't touched his sandwich. For a man with such a craving, his appetite had ebbed fast—but that was probably due to the alcohol. Now he picked it up and took a bite, then set it down quickly.

"And the term for the place is a hospice?" I asked.

"Yes. It's a concept that has been popular in Britain for some time and started to catch on in America in the mid-seventies. Basically what we do is help people who have terminal illnesses live as fully and comfortably as they can until their deaths. The philosophy is that death is merely another stage in human development. It should be met with dignity, and we help our patients to achieve that."

"How does a hospice differ from say, a hospital or a convalescent home?"

"Well, as I said, our patients all have terminal illnesses. We can't—and don't—attempt to cure them. Instead, we try to ease their pain: physically, through special mixtures of drugs that are effective without keeping them doped up. And emotionally, by such policies as encouraging their families to be with them as much as possible. Each patient is assigned a team consisting of a doctor, a nurse, a social worker, and a trained volunteer. The staff and patients grow very close; it's an extremely warm atmosphere."

"It must be an expensive place. I mean, with all those staff members giving individual attention to each patient."

Keller shrugged. "Health care is never cheap." He picked up the sandwich and looked dubiously at it, then took another bite, as if he were afraid of insulting the cook.

"Then most of your patients must be well off."

"Not all of them. We accept insurance plans as well as Medicare and MediCal. And special arrangements can be made."

"Such as?"

"You're very curious about our inner workings." He smiled when he said it, but I sensed a wariness.

I decided to manufacture a personal interest. "I have good reason. My Uncle Jim is very ill. Cancer." In reality, my mother's younger brother was a top touring player on the pro bowling circuit. A couple of times before when I'd needed to fictionalize a relative with a disease or handicap, Uncle Jim had popped into my mind. I had a superstition that saying something bad might make it so, and Jim was the least likely person in the family to succumb to anything.

"That's too bad." Keller gave up on the sandwich and pushed his plate away. "How long has he?"

"The doctors haven't said. The problem is, although he owns his home, he doesn't have much cash. If he wanted to go to The Tidepools, what kind of arrangement could you make with him?"

Keller drained his beer and went to the refrigerator for another. "You say he owns a house? Does he have any other assets?"

"Some rental properties."

"That's simple, then. We'd have him draw up a will, with The Tidepools as beneficiary. At the time of his death, we would have first claim on the estate for the amount owing for his care, plus a carrying charge."

"Carrying charge?"

"To reimburse us for what we'd lost by not having immediate payment."

"I see." I also pushed my half-eaten sandwich away. The conversation had killed my appetite. What Keller had just explained made good financial sense, but it sounded somewhat cold-blooded to me. "Well," I said, "I'll bring it up to my uncle when it seems appropriate. The Tidepools certainly looks like a pleasant place to, um, spend one's last days."

"I can assure you it is."

"I did hear something that makes me leery, though."

"Oh?"

"Another of your former employees—Liz Schaff—hinted there had been some unpleasantness there, just before both she and Jane Anthony left your employ."

Keller frowned. "Unpleasantness?"

"Yes. She wouldn't elaborate, though."

His eyes began calculating rapidly. "When did these women leave The Tidepools?"

"Between eight months and a year ago, I think."

"That explains it."

"Then you know what she was talking about?"

"Yes, but it was nothing, really. I'm surprised she would even bring it up. It had nothing to do with either Miss Schaff or Miss Anthony."

"What was it?"

"A problem with one of the patients. Actually, with a member of the patient's family. I won't go into it, however; it's nothing that's likely to happen again."

For a closed issue, I thought, people were mighty sensitive about it. "Still, I'd like to know, if I'm to recommend The Tidepools to my uncle."

"I assure you, Miss McCone, it was nothing." Keller glanced at his watch and pushed his chair back from the table. "It's after six, and I have an appointment at seven."

I stood up. "Thank you for taking the time to talk to me."

"And thank *you* for demonstrating your excellent culinary skills."

I gave his partially eaten sandwich a skeptical glance and followed Keller down the hall to the front door. As I stepped outside, I remembered some unfinished business. "Oh, by the way, I think you should telephone Ross Brothers, the clothing store, in the morning."

He frowned.

"I don't want to go into it, but your billing address is wrong. You'll want to correct it."

"My billing address?"

"Uh-huh."

A slow smile spread across his puffy face. "This must have something to do with how you located me. The Tidepools would never give out my address."

"You're right."

"But I shouldn't ask."

"Right again."

I left Allen Keller standing on the steps of his house, the bemused smile on his face. The building still reminded me of a house of cards, and I wondered if his messy divorce and the community property laws were what it would take to make it topple.

7

I had two hours before I could catch Don Del Boccio at the radio station after his show. As I drove slowly down the dusk-shrouded streets of Keller's subdivision, I thought about going to my motel, then changed my mind and started north toward Salmon Bay. Sylvia Anthony had said she didn't know Jane's whereabouts, but I didn't believe her. Perhaps I could convince her to tell me or, at the very least, deliver another message from Snelling to her daughter. Possibly I could steer the conversation around to the mysterious trouble at The Tidepools—an unanswered question that was beginning to bother me in much the same way a hangnail does.

When I got to Hydrangea Lane, a light-colored compact was parked in the driveway of the Anthony home. The house itself was dark. I went up to the door, crushing a blue blossom that drooped over onto the steps, and knocked. There was no sound from inside.

I turned and looked over at the car in the driveway, wondering if it might be Jane's. Snelling had said she drove a white Toyota. This was one of those boxy-looking Hondas, but he'd also said that all cars except for VW's looked the same to him. I went down the steps and tried its door. Locked. I peered inside, looking for something that might identify the owner, but the front and backseat were empty.

Turning, I glanced up and down the narrow unpaved street. Lights shone in the other houses and from one of them I could hear the howl of sirens and blare of horns from a TV cop show. Otherwise it was quiet: there were no dogs barking, no children calling, no music or laughter. It was a desolate silence and it made me think fondly of San Francisco's light-hearted vitality.

I left my MG where it was parked and walked through the lanes to the road by the marina. Rose's Crab Shack, a weathered establishment set on stilts over the water, was open, and I went inside. A counter with stools ran along one wall and a couple of rickety tables occupied the rest of the floor space. Hand-lettered signs advertised beer, bait, and burgers.

The only customer was the bearded fisherman I'd spoken to that morning at the boatyard. He glanced at me, then stood up, fumbled some coins onto the counter, and left. A frail old man with shaggy white hair was sitting on a folding chair next to the grill. He raised his head from his newspaper and gave me a cursory look. I ordered a cup of coffee. It was terrible, and I added two spoonsful of sugar, hoping to kill the bitter taste.

I cleared my throat and said, "Interesting little town you've got here." The words sounded ridiculous as soon as they were out.

"No, it ain't."

"I'm sorry?"

"I said it ain't. About the most interesting thing hereabouts is the new fall TV shows, now that we're over the summer reruns."

"Oh."

He picked up his newspaper again. "Of course, today the most interesting thing hereabouts is you."

"What?" I stopped stirring the coffee and set the spoon down.

"I don't know as we've ever had a private detective before. Especially a woman private eye."

"How did you—"

"John Cala told me."

"John Cala?"

"Him, the one that just left."

The fisherman, of course. "But how did he know?"

"Sylvia Anthony. John lives next door."

"Does everybody here know everybody else's business?"

He shrugged. "Why not? Keeps us honest." Then he rustled the paper and disappeared behind it.

I idled away ten minutes, barely touching my coffee. Then I started back to Sylvia Anthony's house, feeling as if the eyes of Salmon Bay were upon me. It was after seven-thirty; if Mrs. Anthony was still out, I'd just go back to Port San Marco and talk to Don Del Boccio.

I was at the corner of the side street that led to Hydrangea Lane when I heard the sound of running footsteps. They were farther up the road, coming toward me from the direction of the old pier. I stopped and made out a bulky figure. As it came closer, I recognized the fisherman, John Cala. I put out a hand to stop him.

"Hey!" I said. "What's going on?"

He pushed my hand away and kept running. As he passed me, I glimpsed his face—it was twisted with fear. He turned into the side street, probably heading for his house.

Now, what was that all about? When I'd talked with him that morning, Cala hadn't seemed a man who would scare easily. But he was plainly frightened. Frightened enough to make me want to know why.

I considered going after him, but decided he'd had too great a head start. After all, I didn't know for certain that he was running for home. Instead, I went on toward the pier. There was no place else out here that he could have been coming from.

It loomed up in the dusk, leaning at an unsteady angle on its pilings. Looking around, I saw no one. I stepped onto the planking and tested it to see how it held my weight. In spite of its appearance, the pier was remarkably sturdy. I started forward, feeling with each step for loose or missing boards. The water sloshed beneath, but otherwise I heard nothing. I got to the end and looked down into the blackness. Here, in the bay, the tide was low. There was nothing frightening down there that I could see. If anything, it was a peaceful place. Far off in the channel I could see a ship's lights. The horizon was a faint line of color, the pinks and reds of the sky paling quickly to indigo. I watched for a moment and then, as I was about to turn to go, I heard a small bumping sound.

I listened. It came again. From under the other end of the pier. I reached into my bag for my small flashlight and started back, shining it through the boards at my feet.

The shape below was pale colored, half in and half out of the water. The part in the water bumped up against the pilings with the motion of the waves. I went over and squatted down on the edge of the planking, shining my light closer. It was a woman, dressed in jeans and a bulky white sweater. She lay on her face on the bank, one arm outflung, her body in the water from the waist down. I sucked in my breath, ran down the rest of the pier, and scrambled over the rocky bank to her.

Her flesh, when I touched her wrist, was cool but pliant. I felt carefully, but could find no pulse. Brushing aside her long dark hair, I touched the spot where the big artery should have throbbed. Nothing. I grasped her shoulder, rolled her on her back.

And looked down into the lifeless face of Jane Anthony.

"No!" I said. The word sounded loud in the stillness.

How had it happened? I picked up my flash from where I'd dropped it next to Jane's body and shone it on her. There was a red stain on the front of the white sweater. She had not fallen from the pier and broken her neck. She had been murdered. Stabbed, maybe. Or shot.

I looked around for a weapon or some other evidence,

but saw nothing. Standing up, I began breathing hard and for a moment was afraid I'd hyperventilate. Police. I had to call the police. Remembering a phone booth in front of the Shorebird Bar, I scrambled back up the bank and started running.

Of course there was no 911 number. The operator, spurred by the urgency in my voice, connected me with the Port San Marco Police. I told them who and where I was, then left the booth. As I waited for the police to arrive, I resisted a strong urge to go into the bar for a drink.

It was ten minutes before I heard the sirens and, by the time the cruiser pulled up, I had been joined by a crowd of weathered men in work clothes who had been inside the bar. I climbed into the police car and directed the officers to the old pier. The crowd followed on foot.

I pointed out where Jane's body lay on the bank beneath the pier, then returned to the cruiser. A plainclothes detective named Barrow spoke briefly with me and said we would talk more later. An ambulance arrived, and lab technicians. The crowd grew larger. After a while I got out of the car and began to pace up and down beside it.

The compact in Sylvia Anthony's driveway must have been Jane's. Yes, Jane had gone to see her mother again. But where was Mrs. Anthony? And why had Jane come here, to the deserted pier? And what about the fisherman I'd met running down the road? Had he found Jane's body? Or had he . . .

The police had set up floodlights and now they illuminated the ambulance attendants as they brought the body up the bank. The crowd moved forward, as if it were one person. The lights' glare picked out eager faces, eyes greedy for a glimpse of the body. Young and old, male and female, they all wore expressions of undisguised anticipation.

My anger rose as I watched them, and I was about to turn away when my eyes met a pair of familiar dark ones. John Cala and I stared at one another for several seconds before he stepped back and vanished into the crowd.

8

As I was leaving the Port San Marco police station at a little after midnight, I saw a plainclothes detective bringing Sylvia Anthony in. They had located her, Lieutenant Barrow had told me, at a church bingo game, and by now she presumably had identified her daughter's body. The police had not been so lucky in finding John Cala. The fisherman was missing from his usual haunts. Barrow had run a check on him, and it turned out he had a record, including a conviction for assault.

Mrs. Anthony's head was bowed and she clung to the plainclothes detective's arm. She seemed frail and even older than she had that morning. When I started over to her, she looked up. Her eyes were red-rimmed but dry, and the bitter lines I'd seen before were deeply set on her face.

She said, "Get away from me."

I stopped.

"Get away," she repeated. "If you hadn't come snooping around here, my girl would still be alive."

The detective raised his eyebrows, shook his head at me, and steered her across the lobby toward the squadroom. I watched them go, then went out to my car. A fine mist hung around the lights in the parking lot and the MG's windshield was covered with saltcake moisture. I got in and turned on the defroster, then sat there waiting for the glass to clear. There was nothing I could do now except go back to my motel and call Snelling. My case was finished—or was it? Maybe he would want me to follow up and see what the police found out about Jane's murder.

When I entered my room I saw that the red message button on the telephone was lit. A sleepy-sounding voice at the desk told me I should call Hank Zahn. It was late, but I knew my boss habitually stayed up until all hours, so instead I dialed Snelling's number. The phone rang and rang, but there was no answer.

Odd, I thought. Where would the reclusive photographer be at almost one in the morning? I dialed again, to make sure I'd called the right number, but the result was the same. Very odd. I pondered it for a moment, came to no conclusion, and called Hank.

He answered immediately, sounded as fresh as if it were nine in the morning. Hank was a restless man whose lean, loose-jointed body needed little fuel other than coffee and the horrible concoctions he whipped up in the All Souls kitchen—and that the other attorneys steadfastly refused to eat. His keen mind thrived on massive doses of information collected from such wide-ranging sources as the newspapers of several major cities, lectures by little-known experts on esoteric disciplines, and advertisements on the backs of cereal boxes. Neither his mind nor his body required much in the way of sleep.

"I just called to see how the investigation's going," he said.

"Not so good."

"How come?"

"The woman Snelling hired me to find is dead. Murdered."

There was a pause. "You do manage to get mixed up in this stuff, don't you?"

"Yes." I'd been involved with six murders in the three years I'd worked for All Souls. Jane Anthony's made it seven. "It's depressing. The victim's mother claims if I hadn't been, as she puts it, snooping around, it wouldn't have happened."

"Do you believe that?"

"No. It was just an emotional statement."

"You don't sound like you don't believe it."

I shrugged, then remembered Hank couldn't see me. "Intellectually, I don't. Otherwise—who knows?"

Hank seemed to sense I didn't want to talk anymore. "Well, I'm sorry it turned out that way. When will you be back?"

"Tomorrow, maybe. After I report to Snelling, I'll let you know."

"Okay." Again he paused. "And, Shar..."

"Yes?"

"Try to get some sleep now."

"Sure. Take care." I hung up and sat on the bed a while, staring at a crack in the beige wall. Then I got up, undressed, and crawled between the sheets.

For a long time sleep wouldn't come. I shifted positions, bunching up the pillows this way and that, trying to clear my mind of images of Jane's lifeless body. When I finally did doze off, I was half-conscious of tossing and turning, coming fully awake in the midst of unclear but disturbing dreams to find myself tangled in the covers, drenched in sweat. As gray light began to seep around the edges of the curtains, I gave up and propped myself against the headboard to think.

I'd certainly never intended my life to take the direction it had. The job with the detective agency that I'd taken after leaving college had been a stopgap measure for an out-of-work sociology graduate who was waiting for her real opportunity to come along. But the flexible hours and freedom from the confining walls of an office suited me; and when the agency had fired me for my inability to bend to authority, my old friend Hank had hired me on at All Souls. The unconventional atmosphere there had suited me even better. I was good at what I did, and proud of it.

If it had stopped there, it would have been fine. Or even if it had stopped with the first murder case, it would have been all right. But there were other deaths, and the older I got the more violence I saw, the more I wondered if I could go on like this indefinitely. And when I wondered that, I also wondered what I would do if I couldn't go on. What on earth *could* a former private eye with a useless sociology degree do for a living?

I got up, took three aspirin, and stepped into the shower. It helped some. When I was dressed I picked up the phone and called Snelling. As before, his phone rang eight, nine, ten times with no answer.

What now? I asked myself. Go back to the city? But what if Snelling—when I finally reached him—wanted me to follow up here? I'd only have to turn around and drive south again. I decided to get some breakfast and then see Don Del Boccio, as I'd planned to before I'd found Jane's body.

The disc jockey was listed in the phone book. He lived in the old section of town, near the harbor. The houses there were great clapboard castles built by the families who had gotten rich during the city's heyday as a fishing port. Now they were broken up into apartments or converted into rooming houses.

I rang Del Boccio's bell and received an immediate answering buzz. Inside was an entryway with scuffed parquet floors and a central staircase. Since none of the doors off the entry opened, I went to the stairs and looked up. A man with a lean, tanned face stared down at me, a mass of black hair falling onto his forehead. When he saw me, his mouth, beneath a shaggy moustache, curved into a wide grin.

"A pretty lady to see me! You've made my morning."

His smile was infectious, and I grinned back. "By saying that, you've made mine."

"You *are* here to see me?"

"If you're Don Del Boccio."

"I sure am. Is this a social call?"

"I wish it were." I told him my name and that I worked for All Souls in San Francisco.

He looked surprised but motioned for me to come up. I climbed to the third floor landing where he stood in an open doorway. He was about six feet tall, a little on the stocky side, and wore faded jeans and a plaid flannel shirt. When I reached the top of the stairs, he gave me a quick appraising look, his hazel eyes moving appreciatively but not offensively over my body. Then he turned and said, "Come on in."

We entered a large, sun-filled room. The far wall was all kitchen, separated from the rest of the space by a bar with stools. An alcove to the right was all bed. The rest of the long room contained a baby grand piano, a set of drums, a stereo, hundreds of records, stacks of books, and a huge blue rug. Large pillows were strewn on its thick pile, but otherwise there was no furniture.

I stood looking around. In spite of the lack of furniture, it was one of the homiest places I'd even seen. If only I could find something half this nice in San Francisco! "This is a wonderful apartment," I said.

"Thanks. Have a seat. I hope you don't mind the floor." He dropped onto one of the pillows. "I just moved in last month, and I'm delighted with the place. I've always dreamed of an apartment where I could gather all the essentials of my life into one room. I can leap from my bed to my piano to my kitchen to my stereo to my drums . . . back and forth, any which way. All with the least possible effort. I like to make the most of my leisure time."

Don Del Boccio was as much of a motor-mouth in person as on the radio—although far more charming. "I know what you mean about leisure time; when you get it, it's precious. And I guess you keep unusual hours, what with your radio show."

He clapped a hand to his forehead in an extravagant gesture of dismay. "Jesus, don't tell me you've heard that!"

"Well, I tuned in for a few minutes yesterday afternoon."

"A few minutes is long enough. It's a terrible show. I hate rock and stupid commercials and teenage callers. I do the whole show wearing earplugs."

"What?"

"Except for the part when I have to talk on the phone and take requests. But as soon as that's over, in go the old plugs."

I laughed, shaking my head. Perhaps that accounted for Del Boccio's noisy style. If he couldn't really hear himself . . . "Good Lord, if you hate it so much, why do you do it at all?"

"Groceries. Rent. You see, I trained as a concert pianist." He rippled his fingers, playing a scale in the air. "Unfortunately, I'm not very good. And actually the job is fun. Nutty, but enjoyable in an odd way."

I'd once had a boyfriend who was a pianist—but he'd ended up a third-rate rock musician. The job market for serious pianists was about as good as it was for sociology graduates. "Where did you go to school?"

"New York. Rochester, specifically. The Eastman School

of Music. I never finished, though; it was so goddamn cold back there that my fingers froze and I couldn't play. So I came back to sunny California and the low-brow life of a deejay."

"But you keep up with your music." I motioned at the piano.

"Yes, ma'am. It's my first love." He paused, studying my face. "But what about you? You said you're a private investigator. What can I help you with?"

I sobered instantly, realizing he probably hadn't heard about Jane Anthony's murder. "I came down here on a missing person's case. An old friend of yours—Jane Anthony."

His mouth twitched beneath the shaggy moustache. "Huh. Janie?" Then his eyes moved from my face to a point beyond my right shoulder. "Funny, I haven't thought about her in a long time."

"You're not close anymore, then?"

"No. We're not exactly what you'd call friends either."

"Why not?"

He shook his head. "Sorry. My business."

"It may not be."

"What is that supposed to mean?"

"Your relationship with Jane may be police business. She's dead."

He jerked his eyes back to mine. "Dead?"

"She was murdered last night, stabbed to death, at the old pier in Salmon Bay."

He flinched. "That can't be."

"I'm sorry, it is."

"Jesus." His face was pained and he looked down at the blue rug. Finally he said, "Who did it?"

"They don't know."

"God. Janie."

"Do you want to talk about her now?"

"There's nothing to talk about. We went together for a couple of years. She was a bright woman, knew about music and art. Had a lot of interests—photography, science fiction. She liked to sail. She was a strong woman. Knew what she wanted in life."

I waited and when he didn't go on, I said, "What was that?"

He raised his eyes to mine. They were moist and sad. "Well, it wasn't me. If it had been, she'd be here with me right now."

"It sounds like you cared a lot for her."

"I guess I loved her."

We sat in silence for a minute, and then I reached for my purse and started to get up. Del Boccio put out a hand. "No, don't go."

"I thought you'd want to be alone."

"No. I'd rather not be. How about if I give you breakfast?"

I'd only had coffee and toast before and, as with Allen Keller's fried egg sandwich, I couldn't resist. Besides, Don Del Boccio might tell me something that would broaden my picture of Jane, give me a clue as to why someone would want to kill her. "All right," I said, "but nothing that's too much trouble."

He jumped up, obviously eager for activity. "You're

looking at one of the world's great cooks, lady. Nothing's too much trouble for Del Boccio."

He went to the kitchen and began rumbling around, carrying on a monologue about his favorite restaurants, both here and in San Francisco. I wondered if he were the sort who felt a need to be on stage all the time, or if this was just his way of diverting himself from Jane's death. Talking nonstop didn't hamper his ability to cook, however; in less than ten minutes he had produced a feast and spread it on a large tray between us on the blue rug. I looked with growing hunger at the scrambled eggs, bacon, bagels, cream cheese, and dry white wine.

"No reason we can't be elegant, even if we are sitting on the floor." He poured wine into delicate stemmed glasses and motioned for me to help myself. Smearing a bagel with cream cheese, he launched into another monologue, this time about Port San Marco.

"Do you like it here? I do, even though the town's changed a lot since I was a kid. It used to be the home of a whole fishing fleet. There were several generations of families who fished these waters. This house was built by one. Those must have been the days, I tell you. But of course, it all changed. Those families couldn't compete with the big companies, and Port San Marco had to turn elsewhere for its bread."

I was about to ask him where, but he went right on.

"Tourism. High-tech firms. The developments you see all over the hills are a consequence of that. Those hills used to be covered with trees and cows and horses—and now look at them. Of course, they're expensive homes and in good taste for the most part. And Port San

Marco's never been in the best of taste anyway. The old amusement park is boarded up now. Going to be torn down and replaced by a performing arts center. I don't mind—I'll enjoy not having to drive to San Francisco for concerts. But, still, I'm going to miss that park. Pinball. Rides. Cotton candy. Saltwater taffy."

He bit into a piece of bacon and I seized my opportunity. "Do you know much about Salmon Bay?"

A look of gloom crossed his face. "We're back to that, are we?"

"I can't help it. It's my job. And you asked me to stay."

"That I did." He smiled ruefully. "You've got to excuse me. Normally I wouldn't babble at you, but . . ."

"I understand."

"To answer your question, yes, I do know Salmon Bay. I was born there. My father was a fisherman, his father too . . . he and my mother still live in Salmon Bay. I don't see much of them."

"Are you on bad terms?" I thought of Jane's relationship with her mother.

"Not really. We don't have much in common, though, and I hate to go up there. The people in the village have a lot of pent-up hate. They blame Port San Marco for surviving commercially while their town failed. They just sit around talking about the good old days and try not to starve. And they resent anyone who has made good. I guess that includes me."

"What about The Tidepools? How do they feel about it being so close by?"

He shrugged.

"Were you seeing Jane when she worked there?"

"At first."

"And then?"

"Then I didn't anymore."

"Do you know about the problems there?"

He ran a finger over his moustache.

"Please, Don. I need to know about it and no one will tell me."

Carefully he poured us more wine. "How did you find out about it?"

"A friend of Jane's who worked there too."

He nodded.

"Will you tell me?"

"Why not? It's no secret." He picked up his glass and leaned back against a pillow, stretching his long legs out. "There was a series of deaths, three of them. Overdoses of the painkilling medicine they use there. With the first two, it appeared the patients had saved up their medication until they had enough to overdose. The staff was blamed for being lax. And, of course, there were the usual rumors."

"Which were what?"

"That someone at The Tidepools had been deliberately lax, had wanted the patients—they were both old women with no living relatives—to die."

"Why?"

"Because they had willed large estates to the place."

I remembered Keller's description of the arrangements that were often made. "You said three deaths, though."

"The third was different. A younger woman with

cancer. It appeared to be a mercy killing by her husband, a medical technician with the Port San Marco hospital."

"Why did they suspect that?"

"He disappeared immediately after. With a lot of money. They've never been able to locate him."

"Sounds more like murder than mercy killing—because of the money."

"Yes."

"Do they think he might have been responsible for the two older women?"

"There was some speculation, but it doesn't seem very likely."

"What about repercussions on the staff?"

"A number of people left afterward, including Jane. The Tidepools wasn't a good place to work anymore."

"But things are better now, at least according to Allen Keller, their director. He said—"

Don sat up straighter. "You know Keller?"

"Not well. Do you?"

"Not well." But his face had darkened and now his eyes grew hard.

"Are you on bad terms with him?"

"I hardly know the man."

"But—"

"I don't know him well, and I don't know anything more about The Tidepools. And, besides, what has Keller got to do with Janie's death?"

"Nothing, as far as I know," I admitted. We finished our breakfast in silence. When I left, Don accompanied me downstairs, tossing off a few comments about some new stereo equipment he was going to take a look at. I got into my car and he squatted down so he could look through the window at me. "Listen, even under the circumstances, I've enjoyed meeting you. Come back, okay?"

"I'd like to."

"I'll make you veal parmigiana."

"Sounds great."

"My lasagna's not bad either."

"You've got a deal."

"I don't usually talk too much."

"I guessed that."

He paused, then squeezed my arm and walked over to an antique Jaguar parked at the curb. It was painted a gauche disc-jockey gold. He got in, started it up, and roared past me, waving.

I liked Don Del Boccio. He was bright and funny and had the kind of good looks that had always attracted me. And right now I wished I were next to him in the gaudy Jaguar, taking a long top-down ride up the coast. Instead, I would have to go back to my motel and try once again to contact Abe Snelling.

9

*B**efore*** calling Snelling I checked with Lieutenant Barrow. He told me they had located John Cala sleeping off a drunk in the parking lot of a bar near the waterfront. The fisherman claimed he'd found Jane's body and then panicked, but Barrow was skeptical of his story.

"What I wonder is why he went out there in the first place," he said. "He claims he was just taking a look around, but there's nothing on that pier, nothing around it."

"Have you established the approximate time of death?" I asked.

"Within an hour of when you found her."

"Could it have been less than fifteen minutes?"

"I doubt it."

"Why?"

"You said in your statement that the body was cool

when you touched it. Even though she was lying half in the water, it's unlikely she would have cooled that much in fifteen minutes. No, I'd say the time of death was closer to an hour before you found her."

"Then Cala probably didn't kill her. I forgot to tell you this last night, but I saw him in Rose's Crab Shack about fifteen minutes before I went out on the pier. He was there, at the counter, and he left as soon as I came in. But he didn't look scared or upset—not like he did when I saw him running away from the pier."

"How come you waited until now to tell me this?"

"In all the excitement I just forgot. I'm sorry."

"Hmmm." There was a pause. "Anybody else in the Crab Shack then?"

"Just the old man behind the counter. He'll verify what I've told you; we even spoke briefly about Cala."

"Thanks. I'll check it out." From what I'd observed of Barrow, he'd be on it right away. He was a seasoned cop, professional as any big-city investigator.

"Is it okay for me to leave Port San Marco?" I asked.

"You heading back to San Francisco?"

"Yes. My job here seems to be done."

"Well, go ahead. I know where to find you if I need you."

I hung up and sat, once more contemplating the crack in the wall. Cala was telling the truth about not killing Jane, but why *had* he gone out on the old pier? I'd have liked to know, but then, it really wasn't any of my concern. The police would get it out of him. I picked up the phone again, hoping Snelling would be at home.

The photographer answered on the first ring. "It's about time you called," he said.

"I tried to, last night and then again this morning. You didn't answer."

"Oh. Of course."

"Where were you?"

"In the darkroom."

"All night?"

"No, of course not. But I like to work in there late at night, and I unplug the phone so if it rings I won't hear it and be tempted to interrupt my work and answer. And I leave it unplugged until I get up, usually around eleven in the morning. What do you have to report?"

"I'm afraid I have bad news." Quickly I told him about Jane's death.

There was a long silence. It stretched out more than thirty seconds. "Abe," I finally said, "are you okay?"

When he spoke his voice was high-pitched and full of fear. "Dead! She can't be dead. How could this happen?"

"Abe, I don't know. But what I can do is stay down here and follow up with the police—"

"No!"

"Obviously you care that someone killed your roommate. Don't you want to find out who it was?"

"It doesn't matter. Don't you see?"

"No, I'm afraid I don't."

"Nothing matters anymore. Nothing. I have to go now, Sharon." There was a click as he set down the receiver.

I hung up and stared at the phone, wondering about Snelling's strange reaction. I had expected regret and sorrow—because he and Jane, while not lovers, had been friends. But what I'd heard was shock verging on panic. Why? I wondered. Because Snelling was not too stable? Or was it something to do with how urgently he had needed to speak to Jane? To find out, I'd have to head back to San Francisco.

It took me only a few minutes to pack and check out, and soon after that I was on the pass road heading inland. Once away from the sea, the air became hot and dry, heavy with the bitter odor of eucalyptus. I opened the car windows and vents to create a breeze. It did little to alleviate the heat, and I kept leaning forward to unstick my shirt from my damp back. The road rejoined the freeway and I sped along on the ridge above the Salinas Valley.

Ten years ago there had been no freeway here, just a winding two-lane road that connected the little valley towns like Bradley, San Ardo, and San Lucas. I remembered Sunday nights, coming back from weekends in Santa Barbara or Los Angeles, when the road would be a continuous line of traffic crawling in both directions. In those days I had thought nothing of driving a six- or eight-hundred-mile round trip on a weekend, but now the prospect was unthinkable. I liked to imagine I was getting more sensible now that I'd entered my thirties, but occasionally I wondered how good that was.

In King City, near the midpoint of the valley, I stopped for gas and a Coke. The soda was sticky-sweet and only made me more thirsty. I leaned against the car as I drank it, watching trucks and autos and campers and buses whiz by on the freeway. A prickly, irritated feeling was rising inside me—both at Snelling for reacting to Jane's death in such an unusual way and at myself for not being able to understand it. I tossed the half-full Coke can in the trash basket and continued north on Route 101, through the ever-present bottleneck at San Jose, up the Peninsula, past the airport, and home.

Watney greeted me vociferously as I entered the apartment. His food bowl was empty, the water dish dry. Tim had obviously forgotten to feed him today. He'd never neglected the cat before, and as I filled the bowls I wondered if perhaps all the beer my building manager guzzled had finally destroyed his few remaining brain cells. The cat taken care of, I got myself a glass of wine—with no consideration at all for my own brain cells—and went into the main room. Everything was the same there—the rumpled quilts, the want ads with the red circles, the books and magazines on the table. I didn't know why I'd expected it to be different, but the lack of change only heightened my sense of discontent.

I tried to call Snelling, hoping he'd calmed down by now. There was no answer. I dialed my service and received two messages—a second one from Paula Mercer about the apartment she'd found for me, and another from my sister, this time leaving her name—Patsy. Patsy was my youngest sister and the family rebel. She lived on a farm up near Ukiah, had three children—each by a different boyfriend—and steadfastly refused to get married. The embodiment of the back-to-the-land craze of the seventies, she sold quilts for money, raised vegetables and chickens for food, and seemed perfectly content to do without TV, video recorders, and electronic games.

Since she had been living like that for eight years and was so good at it, I figured it had passed over the line from being a media-induced aberration to a genuine way of life.

Much as I loved my sister, I didn't want to talk to her tonight. And much as I needed a new apartment, I didn't care to spend the evening looking at one. I ignored both messages and sat, sipping wine, feeling prickly and out of sorts, as dusk fell over the city.

The next morning I drove to the big brown Victorian that housed All Souls. The house was on a steeply sloping side street across from a trash-littered triangular park and, as usual, parking was at a premium. I finally left the MG by a fire hydrant—the meter maids never got there till noon—and hurried up the rickety front steps. The co-op was in its customary morning turmoil: attorneys who didn't live in the second-floor rooms were arriving; others were grabbing their briefcases and rushing off for court. Hank stood by the front desk, talking with Ted, the secretary, about an office-supply order. When Hank saw me, he mumbled something about some documents and notes on my desk. I started down the hall, but suddenly he called after me.

"Abe Snelling phoned me this morning."

I stopped. "What did he have to say?"

"He told me to thank you for your good work and asked that we send a bill."

"How did he sound?"

Hank frowned. "Okay. Why?"

"He was pretty broken up yesterday over his roommate's death."

"Well, he recovers quickly, then. This morning he was all business."

I sighed, irrationally annoyed by Snelling's recuperative powers and went into my office. On my desk was a thick folder of notes on a pretrial conference for a landlord-tenant dispute that was due to go to court next week. I took off my jacket, curled up in my ratty armchair, and spent the next few hours going over it.

The case was an interesting one. A couple had bought a two-unit house with the intention of moving into the upper flat. They'd sold their previous home and were now living in a motel because the occupants of the flat had refused to leave, even after they had been served with a legal eviction notice. Through striking up an acquaintance with the downstairs neighbors, I'd found out that the tenants had already moved into a new apartment and were merely keeping enough possessions in the flat to make it appear they still lived there. They were now attempting to extort several thousand dollars from the new owners before they would remove everything and give up the keys to the premises.

I'd followed the tenants, gotten pictures of them entering their new apartment, and we'd subpoenaed evidence that they'd changed the addresses on their bank and charge accounts. It promised to be a lively court battle, since the tenants were a surly and unpleasant pair, and I was looking forward—in spite of being a renter myself—to testifying against them.

What other work remained for me that day was not

nearly so interesting. My briefcase lay on my desk, fat with documents to be filed at City Hall—one of my less glamorous but important duties. I regarded it with distaste, then left the office and went down the long hall to the big country kitchen at the rear of the house. A couple of attorneys were there, making a salad. I looked into the refrigerator and saw nothing but lettuce, carrots, tomatoes, spinach, and alfalfa sprouts.

"Yuck!" I said.

Anne-Marie Altman, a striking blond who specialized in tax law, looked over at me and grinned. "Too healthy in there for you, huh?"

"You've got it. Why don't you people buy some real food?"

"Like what?"

"Hot dogs. Hamburgers. There are some wonderful new frozen dinners on the market."

She made a face at me and tossed me a radish. I popped it in my mouth and left the room. Back in my office, I sat at the desk, contemplating the full briefcase. There was a McDonald's near the Civic Center. I could stop there for lunch, I thought. But, dammit, I didn't feel like filing documents. If only Jane Anthony's murder and Abe Snelling's initial panic and subsequent cooling of interest didn't nag at me so.

Then I remembered Liz Schaff. I'd promised to let her know what I'd found out. Maybe she could give me some insight into Jane's relationship with Snelling. Surely Jane had mentioned more about her roommate than his name. I picked up the phone, remembered Liz worked afternoons, and called her at home. She agreed to meet me for a quick lunch and suggested the Blue Owl Cafe, across from the hospital.

Liz was sitting at one of the umbrella-covered tables when I arrived, wearing her coat against the chill, the fall sunlight glinting off her bright blond hair. It was one of those crisp, clear days that make up for the summer fog in San Francisco, and the striped umbrellas and flowers on the tables added a further note of cheer.

When I sat down at the table, I noticed that Liz had a glass of wine in front of her. It surprised me to see a nurse drinking before going on duty, but I reminded myself it wasn't as if she was an airline pilot. I ordered wine too, and we both chose cheeseburgers. When the waiter had gone, Liz leaned forward across the table.

"Have you found Jane?"

"In a way."

"What does that mean?"

"I'm afraid your friend is dead," I said gently. "Murdered. I found her body the night before last."

"You found..." Her face went pale and she reached for her wineglass. "Where?"

"Do you know the old pier in Salmon Bay?"

"God, yes. We used to hang out there in high school, to drink beer and neck."

"Well, I don't think she went there for either reason. But someone stabbed her and left her body on the bank, half in the water."

Liz drained her glass and signaled to the waiter, who seemed to know her, for another. She passed a hand over her eyes, as if to brush away tears. "Someone? Don't the police have any idea who?"

"No. Do you know a fisherman named John Cala?"

"Yes. He went to the same high school as we did. He was wild, always in trouble."

"At first the police suspected him. But he's got an alibi."

"Why would they suspect John?"

"He found the body before I did, but didn't report it. He went out on the pier for some reason, but he's not saying why. I'd give a lot to know."

Liz looked thoughtful. "When did this all happen? The other night?"

"Yes. Around eight o'clock."

"And the police arrested John?"

"He's probably been released by now."

"And he won't say what he was doing there?"

"No."

"God. What a mess." She sipped from her fresh glass of wine and a little color returned to her face. "So what else are the police doing about it?"

"The usual things, I would imagine."

"And what about you?"

"I'm off the case. Abe Snelling decided he couldn't use my services anymore."

"I see." Liz paused as the waiter placed our food in front of us. She looked at her burger with unconcealed distaste.

"Liz," I said, "what did Jane tell you about her relationship with Abe Snelling?"

"Nothing, except he was a friend and helping her out."

"She didn't say anything else? How she met him? About his work or their mutual interest in photography?"

"She didn't say anything. I didn't even know he was a photographer until you mentioned it the other night. And of course Jane wouldn't discuss photography with me—she knew I didn't even know which end of a camera to look through."

"How good a friend of Jane's were you?"

"Oh, we were pretty close. We palled around at The Tidepools, had drinks after work. Sometimes we'd have dinner."

"And here, in the city?"

"We saw each other occasionally."

"After the patients died, you left The Tidepools first, right?"

Her eyes widened a little. "So you found out about that."

"It wasn't hard. I gather it was public knowledge."

"Yes, it was." She picked up her burger, took a deliberate bite, and began chewing as if it were hard work.

"The person who told me about the deaths mentioned a drug they use there," I said, "a painkiller that the patients overdosed on."

"Look, I'd rather not talk about it."

"Just tell me about the drug. Then we'll drop the subject." I didn't exactly know why I was prying into the matter of the deaths at The Tidepools, but I had long ago learned to trust my instincts.

Liz sighed and set her burger down. "It's a variation of something called Brompton's Mix, which was developed in England. It consists of morphine, alcohol, and one of the phenothiazines."

"The what?"

"Thorazine, Compazine, or—Look, this can't possibly mean anything to you."

I had to admit it didn't. "It's a strong enough mix to kill a person, though?"

"Obviously, if taken in sufficient quantity. Which the patients did."

"How could they have gotten hold of that much of the drug?"

"The police thought they must have saved it up from their daily dosages." Liz's mouth twisted bitterly. "Of course, they only came to that conclusion after thoroughly grilling the staff. But they could see for themselves that the pharmacist kept tight control over all the drugs. There was no way he would have allowed anyone to get his hands on more than the authorized dosages."

"Did you know any of the patients who overdosed?"

"I knew all three. But I wasn't on the medical team that was assigned to any of them."

"Was Jane?"

"I don't . . ." She paused, a strange look passing over her face.

"Was she?"

"I think so. I'm not sure if she worked with all three of them, but I know she was assigned as Barbara Smith's social worker."

"Which one was Barbara Smith?"

"The last one. The one whose husband . . ." She looked at her watch. "I've got to get to work."

"Liz—"

"I've got to go." She stood up, placing some money on the table. "Thank you for telling me about Jane." Quickly, she strode out of the railed-off cafe. I watched her cross the wide street, her white shoes moving swiftly, her brown coat billowing open to reveal her starched smock and pants.

I looked down at my cheeseburger, then at the briefcase that sat on the floor beside my chair. I should go to City Hall and get those documents filed. I should forget about Jane Anthony and The Tidepools. If it didn't take too long at City Hall, I could spend the remainder of the afternoon hunting for a new apartment.

Instead, I left my lunch untouched and went to Abe Snelling's house.

10

By the time I reached the half-demolished block on Potrero Hill, I'd come up with a strategy for approaching Snelling. Like most artistic people, the photographer had a passion for his work and probably enjoyed talking about it. After all, hadn't he and Jane originally become friends because of her interest in his art? If I could tap into that enthusiasm—and it shouldn't be hard since I was an amateur photographer myself—I might gain enough of Snelling's confidence that he would talk freely about Jane and his urgent need to find her. It might even lead to him reopening the investigation.

The demolition crews were working today and I had trouble finding a place to park. Finally I sandwiched the car between two trucks near the dead end and walked down the street toward Snelling's house. The neighborhood was noisy with the grating sounds of pounding, ripping, and prying. A couple of the workers shouted and whistled at me as I passed, and I smiled at them. More militant feminists than I would have taken offense, but what the hell—some days I could use all the admiration I could get.

I pushed through the gate in the redwood fence and went down the path to Snelling's door, feeling as if I had stepped into a jungle. The palms rustled overhead and amid the tangled vines, bright, mysterious flowers bloomed. I was trying to figure out what they were when the photographer opened the door a crack and looked out over the security chain.

"Sharon." His voice was shaky. "Is anything wrong?"

"No, nothing's wrong. I just want to talk to you."

"Oh." He hesitated and then I heard the chain rattle. When he opened the door, he was running his hand through his thinning blond hair. He looked even more pale than usual, and his thin face was ravaged, as if he'd spent a bad night.

I waited for him to speak and when he just stood there, I said, "I was in the neighborhood, seeing a client and I thought . . ." I paused, surveying his faded jeans and stained shirt, similar to those he'd worn the first time I'd come here. "I guess I caught you in the darkroom."

"Not really." His shoulders drooped with resignation. "I was just cleaning up. Otherwise I wouldn't have come to the door at all. What can I do for you?"

He didn't look in any shape to talk about Jane Anthony, so I began in on the story I'd thought up on the way over here. "Well . . . I'm embarrassed. I shouldn't have dropped in like this. But I thought maybe if you had a little time you'd show me your darkroom and studio. I do some photography myself—not a lot and not very well—and, frankly, I've been dying to see how a real professional operates."

Snelling looked relieved and wary at the same time. "I see."

"I can come back some other time—"

"No, no." He made a dismissing motion with one hand. "I'd be glad to show you." He started off down the hall and I followed.

We went through the living room—where the draperies were still closed in spite of the sunlight—and up the spiral staircase. It led to a large room that was glassed in on the far end, the one that faced the Bay. There were skylights in the roof and the walls were painted the same stark white as downstairs. The room was devoid of furnishings, except for a stool in its center. Shelves on the rear wall held photographic equipment.

I went over there and looked at the cameras. There were three, one of which was similar to mine. "Which of these do you use the most?"

"The Nikkormat."

"That's what I have."

"You like it?"

"Yes, very much. It's light and easy to handle. And when you're as clumsy with a camera as I am, that's important."

"Have you been at it long?" He came over and took the Nikkormat off the shelf.

"Forever, it seems, but I never get any better. I work at it for a while, drop it, then take it up again six months later. When I'm into it, I spend hours and hours in the darkroom at Dolores Park and sometimes I get the feeling I'm improving. But, then, I'll shoot a few rolls and let them sit for months without developing them. I've got film in my camera left over from a visit to my family last May. My mother keeps demanding copies of the photos and I keep putting her off." Surprised at the rush of words, I reined myself in. Snelling was the one who was supposed to be doing the talking.

My monologue seemed to have relaxed him, however. He took the lens cap off the camera and stuffed it into his shirt pocket. "But while you're working at it, you enjoy it, right?"

"Yes."

"And you're not trying to make a living at it."

"Lord, no!"

"So why worry about it?" He walked to the center of the room and took a light meter reading. "Come on over here. I want to get some shots of you. You have interesting bone structure."

I went over to him, and he took another reading, close to my blue sweater. "Sit down." He pointed at the stool. "And don't pose, because if you do, I won't touch the shutter."

I sat, feeling self-conscious. Snelling walked around me, his footsteps light on the linoleum floor. The stool was a swivel type, and I turned to watch him. "You only use natural light?"

"Yes."

"What about a tripod?"

"Sometimes. Depends on what I'm after." He kept moving, watching me through the camera. "Like I said, you have interesting bone structure. Are you Indian?"

"Only an eighth."

"What's the rest?"

"Scotch-Irish."

"What do you think of Stanford's team this season?"

"What?"

Click.

I grinned. "You tricked me."

Click.

"I had to. You were looking at me with a suspicious expression, as if you expected me to pull a gun on you."

"Sorry." I spread my hands out. "I don't like being the center of attention."

Click.

"Well, I suppose in your business it doesn't pay to be."

"Definitely not."

"Tell me about it."

Dammit, this wasn't working. I was supposed to be pumping him and instead he was going to get my life story. Still, talking about the detective business was a natural lead-in to talking about Jane. I began telling him about my days guarding dresses at the department store.

All the while, Snelling circled me, lithe as a cat, almost on his tiptoes. Gracefully he weaved and bobbed, moving here and there, making me turn the stool or crane my neck to follow him. He continued to catch me off guard when he clicked the shutter. It was like being stalked by a playful lion. And, although there was no menace involved, after a while my uneasiness returned. Finally I said, "Do you think we could stop now? I feel kind of hunted."

He grinned, obviously unable to maintain his gloomy mood when immersed in his work, and lowered the camera. "You *are* getting that wary look again."

"I feel like you're stalking me."

A strange expression crossed his face and he went to place the camera on the shelf. "I guess that's what you could say I do to my clients—stalk them."

"Do they all get as uncomfortable as I did?"

"Some of them. But you'd be surprised how many of them love the attention. Come see my darkroom." He opened a door next to the shelves.

I got up and crossed to the doorway. Snelling flipped on a red safelight in the ceiling. It illuminated a row of stainless steel tanks, a huge print dryer, and one of the most sophisticated enlargers I'd ever seen. The table that held it was half white Plexiglas, which could be backlit so you could view negatives and slides on it. Water bubbled softly in the washing tank, where several prints floated face down.

"This is wonderful," I said.

"Go on in." Snelling flipped another switch, turning on regular white light.

I stepped inside and looked at the enlarger, clasping my hands behind my back, not daring to touch it. Snelling leaned against the counter that held the tanks, watching me with amusement.

I said, "I thought I was the only one who washed

prints face down, so the other people using the darkroom wouldn't see how awful they were."

"Once I'm done with something I like to go on to the next without being reminded of what's past."

"Like with Jane?" The words were out before I could stop them.

Snelling's mouth pulled down. "Just what do you mean by that? Is it supposed to be a dig because I've halted your investigation?"

"No," I said quickly, afraid that I'd destroyed our rapport. "Of course not. It just seems a similar situation, that's all. I guess people often approach their work and their personal lives in the same way."

Snelling folded his arms across his chest. "I suppose so. But you have to remember Jane and I weren't all that close. I'm sorry she's dead, but I can't mount a costly crusade to find her killer. That's the police's job."

I nodded. "How did you meet Jane?"

"Uh, I was giving a lecture on photography at S.F. State. She came up afterward and asked some questions. They were more intelligent than what I usually hear, so I asked her to have a drink with me. And we became friends."

"And then she moved in with you?"

"Yes, when she couldn't continue to pay the rent on the room where she was living. We lived quietly and companionably until she disappeared."

"Did you have many mutual friends?"

"No. We went our separate ways."

"Did she ever talk about her past, before she came to San Francisco?"

His frown deepened. "Sharon, what is this?"

"I'm curious. I found her body. I feel some sort of . . . I don't know, call it a connection."

He straightened up and started for the door. I went after him.

"Abe, did Jane ever mention The Tidepools?"

He turned, his face lit by the brightness from the studio.

"Did she ever mention The Tidepools?" I asked again. "Or Allen Keller? Or Ann Bates?"

"No." Curtly he motioned me out of the darkroom and began herding me toward the stairs.

"What about Don Del Boccio? Or a fisherman named John Cala?"

"I've never heard of either of them." He was right behind me, his body forcing me down the spiral staircase so fast that I almost stumbled.

"What about a patient at The Tidepools named Barbara Smith?"

We had reached the bottom of the stairway. Snelling blocked my way into the living room, urging me down the hall instead. "Who are all these people? What do they have to do with Jane?"

"Some are former employers. Don Del Boccio was her boyfriend at one time. I don't know about Cala—he lives next door to her mother. I don't know about Barbara Smith either, except . . ."

Snelling unchained the front door and opened it wide. "Except what?"

"Except . . ." I paused, one foot over the threshold. "Except I think Jane may have killed her."

It had only occurred to me at that moment and it was a wild thrust in the dark, but it hit Snelling hard. His pupils dilated and he went even paler. Then he reached out a hand and shoved me through the door.

"Get out of here," he said, "and don't ever come back."

11

*A**nother*** unpleasant confrontation awaited me at All Souls. As I came through the front door, I ran into Hank. His eyes, behind his thick, horn-rimmed glasses, went from my face to the still-bulging briefcase in my hand.

"You didn't file those documents yet."

"Uh, no."

He looked at his watch. "It's nearly four-thirty. What have you been doing all afternoon?"

In truth, I couldn't tell him. After I'd left Snelling's I'd stopped at the McDonald's near City Hall for a hamburger to make up for the one I hadn't eaten at lunch. I'd sat there on the upper deck and watched the traffic on Van Ness Avenue, occasionally reminding myself that I should be going about my business. But the mental prodding had done no good and, after three cups of coffee and two hours of meandering thoughts about Jane

Anthony and Abe Snelling, I'd packed it in and gone back to the office.

"I had some other business to attend to," I said lamely.

"Sharon, those documents are important."

"I know."

"So why didn't you take care of them?"

"Something came up."

"Sharon, this isn't like you."

"I'm sorry."

"That's all you have to say—you're sorry?"

I felt a flush of irritation. "What do you want me to do, kneel and beg forgiveness?"

"You could at least explain—"

"Look, Hank, I've had a bad day." I started to push past him. "The documents will be filed first thing tomorrow."

He blocked me. "It was important some of them be filed today."

"Then why didn't you . . ." I stopped, realizing that what I was about to say was unrealistic, to say nothing of petty.

"Then why didn't I what?"

I was silent, feeling sullen and totally in the wrong.

"Why didn't I file them myself? Is that what you were going to say?" Hank's bony frame loomed over me. Usually my boss was as mild-mannered as they come, but he couldn't tolerate people shirking their responsibilities.

"Look, Hank, just forget it."

"Why didn't I file them myself? My God, Sharon, I'm a *lawyer*!"

The conversation was bordering on the absurd. "Don't lawyers file documents?"

"Not when they have someone on salary to do it!" He waved his hand wildly and almost poked me in the eye. "Not when they pay someone else to handle it."

Why couldn't I have kept my mouth shut? Why had I made it worse? "Drop it, Hank. Please drop it."

He glared down at me, then moved around me toward the door.

"Where are you going?" Hank never left the office before six.

"Out."

"Yes, but where? I might need to talk to you before I go home."

He paused, his hand on the doorknob. "You are not the only one who has had a bad day. I am going down the street to the Remedy Lounge, where I will have a couple of Scotches and contemplate my problems in silence."

"No one has that hard a day. The Remedy Lounge is the sleaziest bar in Bernal Heights, maybe in the entire city."

"Ah, but it has its advantages."

"Which are?"

"It is dark, nearly always deserted, and—best of all—you are not likely to follow me there." He went out, slamming the door for emphasis.

I sighed and went down the hall to my office. Hank was wrong; whether it was sleazy or not, I planned to join him at the Remedy Lounge in a very few minutes.

But before I did that, I wanted to call a friend at San Francisco State, to see if Abe Snelling had ever given a lecture on photography there.

My friend, Seamus Dunlap, was temporarily out of his office. Tapping my fingers impatiently on the desk, I waited for him to call back. He was a color photographer who did work for classy magazines like *National Geographic* and, in fact, the person who had interested me in photography when I'd been dating him years before. If anyone would know about Abe Snelling, it was Seamus.

My phone buzzed and I answered it. "Sharon! How you doing?" Seamus' deep voice seemed to fill my tiny office.

"Pretty good. You?"

"Can't complain."

"Seamus, I have a question for you."

"Shoot."

"To your knowledge, has Abe Snelling ever lectured at State?"

"Abe Snelling." He paused. "Not that I know of. Why?"

I ignored his question. "If he had, within the past year, you would know, right?"

"Does anything ever go on here that I don't know about?"

I chuckled. "Occasionally, as I recall." About a year before I'd met him, Seamus' wife had run off with one of his students. The photographer had been so caught up in his work that he hadn't even noticed for a week.

"Come on, that was centuries ago. Speaking of centuries, when are you and I going to get together?"

"Later this month, maybe." Seamus was attractive and intelligent, but difficult to get along with for any length of time. After Greg Marcus, another temperamental man was exactly what I didn't need.

"Just as easy to pin down as ever, eh? But back to your question: as far as I know, Snelling's never lectured here—or anyplace else. Not that we wouldn't love to have him; but the guy's a recluse."

That was what I'd expected. So why had Snelling lied to me?

"Thanks, Seamus," I said.

"Hey, why are you interested in Snelling?"

"I'll tell you when we get together."

"I'll call you." He probably would, too—a year from now, when he remembered he was supposed to.

"Buy you a drink?"

I slipped onto the cracked vinyl stool next to Hank. He was hunched over the bar, a glass that I knew contained Scotch and soda in front of him. As usual, the Remedy Lounge was dark and empty. The glasses on the back bar were spotted, the mirror fly-specked, and the bartender had a large, nondescript stain across the front of his apron.

Hank looked sidelong at me, then back at his glass. "That's okay. I'll buy."

"But it's a peace offering."

"So's mine."

Since he'd insisted, I ordered bourbon and water. The

bartender plunked the glass down in front of me, and some of the drink slopped over.

"I'm sorry about those documents," I said. "I was preoccupied and time just got away from me. I'll file them first thing in the morning."

He nodded.

"I seem to have a lot of trouble keeping on top of things lately," I went on. "Maybe I need a vacation."

"Probably."

I leaned forward on the bar, laid my hand on a sticky place, and pulled it back. "So I was thinking—could I have a few days off? The tenants' dispute doesn't go to trial until next week and, once I file that stack of documents, I really don't have anything else pending."

Slowly Hank turned to look at me.

"With the weekend, I could get away for around five days. It might do me some good."

"Where were you thinking of going?"

"Oh, I don't know." I sipped my drink. "Maybe back to Port San Marco. I really enjoyed it there; I hadn't been there, you know, for years and years. It's still warm enough to sit on the beach and I could—"

"Uh-huh."

I ignored his skeptical look. "I could relax."

"Right."

"Well, I have to admit there's more to it."

"I guessed as much."

"I met a man there."

"Oh, yeah?"

"Yes. His name's Don Del Boccio. He's a disc jockey, but he's also a classical musician. He has the most wonderful apartment, and this horrible metallic gold Jaguar and . . ." I let the words drift off, realizing that Hank had seen through me for sure now. I never discussed my private life with him if I could help it—which was one reason why it fascinated him.

"Right," Hank said again.

"Well, I *did* meet such a person."

"I didn't think you could make someone like that up. But you also stumbled onto a murder."

"True."

Hank signaled for another drink. "Shar, didn't Snelling say the investigation was closed?"

"Yes, but—"

"You can't just go down there and snoop around without a client."

"I'm not going to 'snoop around.'"

"What *do* you call it?"

"Look, Hank, I've been straightforward with the Port San Marco police. I've given them everything I know and they've appreciated it. I wouldn't go back there without checking in with the lieutenant in charge of the case."

"And what would you tell him?"

"That I was back in town and . . ."

"And what?"

"And that I was interested in hearing whatever they'd come up with."

"Would you tell him Snelling was no longer employing you?"

"He probably wouldn't ask."

"So you'd imply you still had a client."

"I guess you can say that."

"Sharon, it's too risky. You've gotten in trouble with this sort of thing in the past."

"That was before."

"Before what?"

I finished my drink. "I'm more sensible now."

"More sensible than you were last year?"

"Yes. I promise, I'll talk to Lieutenant Barrow first thing. And I'll report anything I find out immediately. Please, Hank, let me have the time off."

He stared down at his glass. "I don't suppose I can stop you. You could always call in sick if I said no."

"Would I do that?"

"Yes." He looked at me, and then the laugh lines around his eyes crinkled. "Ah, what the hell. Go. With my blessing. Maybe you'll come back less of a grump."

"A grump?"

"In case you haven't noticed, you've been impossible the last few weeks."

"Well, I told you I needed a vacation."

We finished our drinks in silence and then Hank said, "I've got to get back to the house."

I stood up. "I'll come with you and pick up my briefcase. If it's okay with you, I'll just file the documents and take off without coming in tomorrow morning."

He slid off the barstool, looking uncomfortable.

"That is all right—just to file them and go—isn't it?"

"Uh, sure."

"What's wrong then?"

He paused. "Nothing, really. Come on."

When we entered the big brown Victorian, I understood what had made Hank hesitate. Greg Marcus sat on an edge of the front desk, chatting with Ted. I supposed Greg and Hank had dinner plans; the two of them had been friends years before I had entered their lives and I couldn't expect that to change now.

When Greg saw me, there was a barely perceptible hardening in his eyes and the lines of his jaw grew taut. Then his face smoothed and he said, "Hi, papoose." To Hank, he added, "You're late."

"I'll only be a minute." Hank hurried off down the hall without so much as a glance at me.

Ted, craven coward that he was, got up and muttered something about the men's room.

I turned to Greg. "So, how have you been?"

"Okay. How about you?"

"Busy. I've been hunting for a new apartment, but without much luck."

"Hank tells me you found a body down near Port San Marco the other night."

Now why had Hank done that? "Yes."

"Up to your old tricks?"

"What tricks?"

"Well, I hope you're cooperating with the police down there better than you've cooperated with me in the past."

For a moment when I'd seen him sitting there, handsome in his blue suit and striped tie, I'd felt a momentary softening. But now all the reasons I'd ended our relationship came flooding back.

"Cooperation," I said, "has to be mutual if it's to

work properly.'' In the instant before I turned and started down the hall, I saw him do a double take.

Greg, however, could not be humbled for long. ''Always quick with the snappy comeback, eh, papoose?''

I kept going, into my office. No wonder I had broken up with him! No wonder. Besides, what kind of woman could remain in love with a man who called her by such a ridiculous nickname?

12

I was back in Port San Marco, in the same room at the Mission Inn, by three the next afternoon. As soon as I'd unpacked, I called Lieutenant Barrow at the police department. The investigation of Jane's murder was going slowly, he told me, and they were now in the process of interviewing her friends and former neighbors and employers. John Cala had been released; he still insisted he'd merely gone out on the pier for a stroll and, while Barrow didn't believe him, the alibi I'd supplied for the fisherman had checked out.

"So that's where we stand at present," Barrow said. "This one isn't going to be easy."

"You seem to be acting on the theory that the killer was someone out of Jane's past."

"It stands to reason. She was killed in Salmon Bay, in a place that few people from outside the area would know about."

"She could have arranged to meet an outsider there."

"Possibly." But he obviously didn't think much of the idea because he changed the subject. "I take it you're back in town?"

"Yes. I'd like to ask your permission to follow up on a few leads. Of course, I'd report my findings immediately."

"What kind of leads?"

"Nothing earthshaking. I'd like to talk to Jane's mother again, and possibly John Cala."

"If you can get anything out of either of them I'll be very surprised. The people in that damned village are as close-mouthed as they come."

"So I've noticed. But I'd like to try anyway. Also, I want to talk to the people at The Tidepools. I suppose you investigated the deaths there?"

There was a pause. "Yes, but I don't see any connection."

"Jane worked there at the time."

"I know that; we've already checked with their personnel director, Ann Bates. But the deaths are a closed file, except for the last one, where the husband apparently did the killing and then disappeared."

"I'd still like to look into a possible connection."

"Go ahead, if you want. But I doubt you'll find one."

"But it's okay with you?"

"Sure. Just keep in touch."

As I'd expected, he hadn't asked me if Snelling was still my client. I hung up, found the address of the public library in the phone book, and set off to check their back issues of the Port San Marco *Herald*.

* * *

At five-o'clock I rewound the last reel of microfilm and left the redwood-and-glass building that housed the library, rubbing my eyes. The first death at The Tidepools, of a seventy-eight-year-old patient named Mary Sloan, had been perfunctorily reported as a suicide. With the second, of an eighty-three-year-old woman named Amelia Canfield, the reporter had indulged in speculation that the drug overdoses had been connected. A small item appeared weeks later, stating that both deaths had been ruled suicides. Two months later, Barbara Smith's death had received front-page coverage.

Mrs. Smith had been in her early thirties, suffering from terminal cancer. She had been at The Tidepools barely three weeks when she was found dead, an apparent overdose like the others. What distinguished her death from theirs, however—besides the obvious difference in age—was that she hadn't been at the hospice long enough to have saved up a lethal dose of the painkiller. In fact, she hadn't been receiving the mixture for more than a few days. And, immediately after her death, her husband, Andy, a medical technician with Port San Marco General Hospital, had vanished.

The reporter had talked to Barbara Smith's friends and relatives. She had been in good spirits, they said, and was happy to have been admitted to The Tidepools. Besides, she wasn't the type to kill herself. I myself tended to discount their statements. If you believe the friends and relatives, no one who commits suicide is the type to do it. What I didn't discount was the fact that two months before her death Barbara Smith had received an inheritance of more than forty thousand dollars, which should have gone to pay for the cost of her lengthy care at the hospice. Her husband had withdrawn the money in cash from their joint savings account several days before she died—and he left town in a hurry.

The story had continued to receive coverage for a week after Barbara Smith's death but, when the police failed to locate her husband, it had faded into obscurity. Probably Smith would never be found; forty thousand dollars could buy of lot of anonymity.

I went back to my motel, put on my swimsuit, and went out to the pool. Swimming was the one sport I really enjoyed—far more than the tedious workouts I endured weekly at my neighborhood health club—and it also relaxed me and helped me think. I was firmly convinced there was some mysterious connection between water and the creative process: I knew writers who wrote in the bathtub, businessmen who plotted strategy in the shower, actors who worked on their lines in the hot tub. As for myself, I puzzled out cases in swimming pools.

I eased into the unheated water and began swimming. Up, down, across, back, laps, lengths. Sidestroke, crawl, breaststroke, butterfly. I was getting plenty of exercise, but after a while I realized nothing else was happening. The facts of the case failed to form any rational pattern.

Jane Anthony had been missing for a week and then someone had stabbed her to death. . . . She had been killed in an out-of-the-way place few people except for residents of Salmon Bay would ever know about. . . . The man who first discovered her body had no good reason for being in that place. . . . Abe Snelling had panicked after hearing of Jane's death, then called a halt to my investigation. . . . Snelling had also lied to me about how he met Jane. . . . There had been three deaths at The Tidepools while Jane had worked there, all of them suspicious. . . . Jane had been assigned to the medical team that had worked with at least one of those patients. . . .

I needed to find out why John Cala had gone to the old pier. I needed to find out if Jane had been assigned to the other women who had died of overdoses at The Tidepools. I needed to find out how Jane really met Snelling.

I got out of the pool and went back to my room. While blow-drying my hair, I planned a course of action. I would go to see Mrs. Anthony and John Cala. And tomorrow I would convince either Ann Bates or Allen Keller to let me look at The Tidepools' records on Jane. Probably the police had already done so, but they hadn't been looking for the same thing I was.

When I arrived in Salmon Bay, the Anthony home was dark. After knocking and getting no response, I asked an old man who was mowing his lawn which house was John Cala's. He pointed to the one to the right of Sylvia Anthony's. It was small and box-like and had once been painted a light green, but the color had faded and now the paint was beginning to peel. Cypress trees hunched on either side of it, their branches drooping onto its flat roof. The unfenced front yard contained an assortment of junk: tires, lumber, plastic milk crates, old mattresses, rolls of chicken wire, and a washing machine without a lid. I'd noticed the place before, mainly because it presented such a contrast to Mrs. Anthony's flower-filled yard. I decided it fit with my impression of Cala. I made my way through the jumble to the front door and knocked but got no answer. Either Cala and Sylvia Anthony weren't home, or they weren't in the mood to welcome callers.

I went back to the MG and started it, uncertain of what to do next. Glancing at my watch, I flipped the radio to KPSM Don Del Boccio was dedicating a song from Sally to Larry and urging listeners to call in on the Hot Hit Line. I drove to the Shorebird Bar, got out a dime, and went into the phone booth.

"Hot Hit Line," Don's voice said. "What can I play for you tonight?"

"I doubt you've got anything there I'd want to listen to. It's Sharon McCone. Can I buy you a drink after your show?"

"You sure can. I was hoping you'd get in touch. How about eight-fifteen at the Sand Dollar? It's on Beach Street, by the marina."

I'd seen the place. "All right. See you then." I went back to the car and started off toward Port San Marco, feeling much more cheerful. As I turned up the radio, a tire commercial ended and Del Boccio, in a softer voice than he usually employed, dedicated a song to Sharon from Don. It was James Taylor's "You've Got a Friend."

The Sand Dollar faced the water where the charter fishing boats tied up. It was a brightly lit place with tables on levels separated by shiny brass railings. Old-fashioned fans stirred the fronds of giant ferns that hung nearby. This type of fern-bar modern decor usually indicated a singles' bar, but the Sand Dollar had none of that frantic, clutching atmosphere. I took a table on the top level, from where I could see the lights of a ship in the channel, and ordered a glass of wine.

Don came through the door promptly at eight-fifteen. He spotted me and started across the room, waving to people on either side, giving a thumbs-up signal to the bartender, shaking hands with one of the waiters. He wore jeans and a rough cotton shirt that was unbuttoned just enough to show a couple of inches of thickly haired chest. I watched his easy progress with pleasure, smiling in response to his obvious good cheer. To look at him, you'd never know he'd been talking, yelling, and making strange honking noises for six hours. When he arrived at the table, a waiter was right behind him with a glass of red wine.

"I take it you're a regular here," I said.

He flopped into the chair, reaching for his wine. "Sort of. When they see me coming, they know it's been a rough night and they do their best to ease my pain." He raised his glass to me, winked, and downed half the wine.

"And has tonight been a rough one?"

"You've heard the show, babe—they all are." But as he said it, he grinned. I had the feeling that nothing was really all that disagreeable to Don.

He leaned back in his chair, studying me over his wineglass. "So, I take it you're investigating Jane's murder, since you're still here. I've kept up on it through the people in our news department and it doesn't sound like the police have found out much."

"Nothing too promising."

"I guess your client has more confidence in you than in them. Who did you say he was?"

"A photographer named Abe Snelling, Jane's former roommate. But he's not my client anymore."

Don frowned.

"He decided when she died that the case was closed. I went back to San Francisco after I saw you last, but I couldn't get my mind off the murder, so I came back down here on my own."

He set his glass down and ran a finger over his bushy moustache. "Poor Jane. The guy doesn't even care who killed her. She never did have much luck with men. Is this Abe Snelling a boyfriend, or what?"

"Mostly what. He claims they were just friends, and not very close at that. But a few days ago he was awfully anxious to find her, and he lied to me about how they met. When you say Jane never had much luck with men, what do you mean?"

"She kept making the wrong choices—guys who treated her badly; guys who were weak and leaned too heavily on her; guys with messy domestic situations."

"I take it you don't include yourself in those categories."

"Me?" He grinned and sat up straighter. "I'm a fine catch. A terrific cook, in the best of health, self-supporting, don't leave my underwear on the floor, thoroughly domesticated. You could do worse."

"I'm sure I could." The silence that fell between us was not uncomfortable, merely speculative. Finally I said, "Well, tomorrow I'm going to get answers to some of the questions about Jane that have been bothering me."

"Such as?"

"Her connection with those deaths at The Tidepools. I'm going up there and talk to Allen Keller—"

A look of intense dislike flickered in Don's hazel eyes and he attempted to mask it by picking up his glass and motioning to the waiter for refills. He'd reacted to Keller's name that way the first time I talked to him.

"What is it with you and Keller?" I asked.

"What do you mean?"

"You really don't like him. Why?"

He sighed. "It shows that much, does it?"

"Yes."

"Well, if we must talk about him, Keller was one of the guys Jane got mixed up with, one of the ones with a messy domestic situation. It was my misfortune to be the guy she dumped when old Allen came along."

So Keller, like Snelling, had lied to me about Jane. "I see. Keller told me he was getting divorced. . . . What exactly was his situation when Jane became involved with him?"

The waiter brought two fresh glasses of wine and Don waited until he had left before speaking. "Keller was married to his third wife, Arlene. He had a reputation as a womanizer—that's how he ended up with wives number two and three—but Arlene kept him on a tight leash, at least until Jane came along."

"And then?"

"At first Allen and Jane were pretty discreet. Hell, *I* didn't even know about it for months, and I lived in the same apartment complex and still saw her regularly. They would meet at the marina over there." He gestured at the window. The marina was well lit, the forest of boat masts white against the dark sky.

"He has a boat there?" I asked.

"A cabin cruiser. Arlene never liked it or the people at the marina, and they didn't like her. It was a safe place for Allen and Jane to go. But then they decided they were in love and once they decided that they couldn't keep it quiet. Jane broke off with me. She asked me not to tell anyone about Allen, and I didn't. Allen began squirreling away assets, because of the community property laws. He didn't want Arlene to have her share."

I remembered what Keller had said to me about having made the money and it being his.

"That would have been okay," Don went on, "but Allen also started taking Jane out in public. He made a lot of stupid moves, like renaming the boat *Princess Jane*. People started to talk. This is a small town, in spite of the way it's grown in the past ten years. It wasn't long before Arlene knew the whole story."

"And she filed for divorce?"

"Yes. And because Arlene knew Allen had manipulated his finances when he split from his second wife, she hired detectives to trace their joint assets. They found he'd forged Arlene's signature a couple of times, and she demanded a huge settlement in exchange for not prosecuting. I gather Keller had to liquidate a number of holdings in order to keep her from getting her hands on The Tidepools. Rumor has it he's on the verge of bankruptcy."

I recalled the impression I'd had of Keller's home as a house of cards. "What happened with him and Jane?"

"She couldn't take the heat of the scandal. Quit her job at The Tidepools and moved to San Francisco. But she still saw Keller—they were in here together last month—and I think they hoped it would work out for them once he got his financial affairs in shape. And it probably would have; the scandal would have eventually died down. People give up, you know, when there's nothing fresh and juicy to chew over."

"You say you saw Keller with Jane last month?" If she had been with him then, she could also have been with him the past week.

"I didn't, but someone from the station did and, of course, she felt she had to mention it."

"Has anyone seen them together since then?"

"Not that I know of."

I'd have to have a talk with Keller tomorrow, I decided. Suddenly tired, I drained my glass and looked at my watch.

Don said, "Can I cook dinner for you one night this week? It would have to be after eight, of course. I'm happy having the show in a prime time slot, but it doesn't allow for a normal social life."

"That's okay; I've never had one of those myself. And, yes, I'd love to have dinner."

He grinned, the motioned to the waiter for the check. Our departure from the restaurant was accompanied by the same waving and handshaking as Don's arrival had been, and I realized he was something of a local celebrity. When I commented on the fact, however, he shrugged and said, "It's a friendly town." His offhandedness made me like him even more.

We walked toward my car, Don's hand resting lightly on my arm. As we came in sight of the MG, I spotted a figure in dark clothing leaning down next to it, as if trying to see through the window.

"Hey!" I called.

The figure moved back onto the sidewalk, behind a group of people who stood talking in front of a restaurant. I shook off Don's hand and quickened my pace. The figure started to run, and I went after it.

A tourist couple came out of the restaurant. They were both fat, and the man had his arm around the woman. I dodged to the left, but a kid on a skateboard came zooming by, barely missing me. The couple both seemed tipsy; when they tried to avoid me, they staggered and then stopped. The woman giggled and the man smiled apologetically. By the time I'd gotten around them, the dark figure had vanished.

Don came up behind me. "What was that about?"

"I don't know." I turned and hurried back to my car. Both doors were locked and the convertible top was intact, but I got out my keys, opened the passenger door, and unlocked the glove box. The .38 Special I kept there had not been touched.

I straightened up and turned to Don. His mouth was open and he was looking at me as if he were seeing me for the first time. "You're for real, aren't you?" he said.

"What?"

He motioned at the glove box. "It's one thing hearing you talk about an investigation, but seeing that..."

I smiled. After dating a cop who took things like the .38 for granted, I'd forgotten how it could scare off potential boyfriends. "Don't worry." I put my hand on Don's arm. "I've very rarely had to use it."

He covered my hand with his and squeezed it. "But you do know how."

"Yes. I wouldn't own it if I didn't." The image of a man I'd once killed flashed into my mind, but I shook it off, as I always did. I certainly didn't want to go into that with Don—not until I knew him a lot better.

He smiled. "Well, just don't bring the gun to dinner."

"I'll bring wine instead."

We exchanged phone numbers—mine at the motel, his at home—and said good-night there on the sidewalk. Intrigued as I was by the prospect of a budding romance with this attractive man, my thoughts were on the figure I'd seen by my car. It could have been nothing, but I'd do well to be more alert in the future. And the romance, I told myself as I drove back to the Mission Inn, would have to wait until I cleared up the business at hand.

13

At ten the next morning I sat on one of the ornately carved chairs in the lobby of The Tidepools, waiting to talk to Ann Bates. I'd been there half an hour and the high-backed chair grew harder with each passing minute. Every time I shifted my position, the handsome dark-haired woman at the desk would look up, an anxious frown creasing her brow. When I finally stood up and went over to the glass wall that opened onto the patio, the woman jerked. I glanced curiously at her, but she lowered her eyes.

The hospice seemed strangely hushed this morning. Except for the woman at the desk, I hadn't seen a single soul, and the phone hadn't rung once all the time I'd been waiting. Even the fountain was quiet, its water turned off, and not a breeze ruffled the fuchsia blossoms in their hanging baskets. It wasn't a peaceful stillness, however.

The receptionist's tension had begun to affect me. When the carved front door opened, squeaking on its iron hinges, I jumped. A middle-aged couple, prosperous-looking in tweeds, came in. They conferred with the receptionist, then took seats on the far side of the lobby. Tired of waiting, I went over to the woman at the desk and asked how much longer Mrs. Bates would be.

"Oh, I'm certain it won't be more than a few minutes." She did not meet my eyes.

"Would you get her on the phone again and find out?"

Her hand strayed toward the receiver, then stopped. "She knows you're here. I'm sure she'll be out as soon as she's free." She looked up, and I saw that her eyes were almost pleading. Obviously Bates was the source of her jumpiness.

I said, "Is she in a bad mood today?"

A smile tugged at the corners of the woman's mouth. "Today and yesterday. All week, in fact. I'd rather not bother her again—" Footsteps clicked on the tiled floor behind us and the trace of a smile disappeared from the woman's lips.

I turned to face Mrs. Bates. Dressed in beige silk, she was as fashionable as the last time I'd seen her, but there were lines around her mouth that hadn't been there before. "Ms. McCone," she said, "what can I do for you?"

"I take it you've heard about Jane Anthony's death?"

"The police were here making inquiries. And of course it was in the papers."

"I'm cooperating with the local force in the investigation, and there are some questions I need to ask you."

"I've already told the detectives from Homicide everything I know about Ms. Anthony. Perhaps you should talk to them."

"No, I'd rather talk to you."

Bates glanced at the couple on the other side of the lobby, and then at the receptionist. "Mary, who are—"

"Relatives of a prospective patient. One of the volunteers is to give them a tour, but she hasn't arrived yet."

Bates frowned. "Doesn't she know enough to be on time, for God's sake?"

"They're early."

"Well . . . oh, never mind." Bates looked back at me, exasperation plain on her face. "Ms. McCone, I realize you are merely trying to do your job, but you are hindering me from doing mine. As I said before, I suggest you talk to the police."

Her voice was louder now, and the prosperous-looking couple turned their heads. I raised my own voice. "You also must realize that by refusing to talk to me you're obstructing my investigation of this murder."

The man sat up straighter and he and the woman exchanged looks.

"Ms. McCone!" Bates glanced at them frantically.

"Since you won't talk with me I can only assume that you—or someone else at The Tidepools—have something to hide."

Two spots of red appeared on Bates' cheeks. She heaved a sigh and said to the receptionist, "Hold all my calls, Mary." Then she glared at me. "Come this way, Ms. McCone." In icy silence we went down a hallway to an office wing.

Bates led me into a paneled office with a view of a cypress grove. It was furnished with a large, cluttered desk and banks of metal filing cabinets. She made a curt motion at a visitor's chair in front of the desk, then went around and sat behind it.

"Now that you have succeeded in making both me and The Tidepools look bad," she said, "what do you want to ask me?"

"I need to see Jane Anthony's personnel file."

"Absolutely not."

"Why?"

"It's confidential."

"The woman's been murdered. Nothing about her is confidential anymore."

"The file is the property of The Tidepools."

"'Did you refuse to show it to the police?"

"They didn't ask. They merely questioned me about what I recalled about Ms. Anthony."

"All the more reason I should see it."

She leaned forward on the desk, her eyes flashing. "No, Ms. McCone. All the more reason you should not. If the police didn't need to see the file, you don't either."

This statement was going to be broken only by the introduction of a new element. "Why don't we get Allen Keller in on this?"

She blinked and took her elbows off the desk. "I thought Mary told you when you arrived that Dr. Keller isn't in today."

"Has he been in at all since Jane Anthony was killed?"

"That's none of your business." But the fire went out of her eyes and she bit her underlip.

"I guess he's taking it hard. It would be a shame to have to disturb him over something like this file."

"Yes, it would."

"On the other hand, if I have no choice . . ."

"Ms. McCone, Allen—Dr. Keller has had a very difficult time this week. He told me how you hunted him down at home."

"Did he also tell you that he lied to me about how well he knew Jane?"

"That's only natural, given the havoc that woman wreaked upon his life. I don't want you bothering him any more."

"But I need to see that file."

She was silent, her hands gripping the arms of her chair. Her face, which had seemed invulnerable moments ago, was now deeply troubled. I thought of women I'd known who had fallen in love with bosses or co-workers. They might lose them to other women, but still they went on, keeping the office fires burning, waiting for some improbable future chance. Was Ann Bates . . . ?

A look of resolve spread over her features and she stood up, taking a key out of her desk drawer. "If I let you see the file, will you leave Dr. Keller alone?"

"Would I have any other reason to contact him?"

"Of course not." Either she was not as bright as she appeared to be or she badly wanted to believe she was doing the right thing. She went to one of the file cabinets, opened it, and reached inside. Then her back straightened and she began to shuffle through the files.

She closed the drawer, opened the one below it, and repeated the procedure. When she finally turned to me, her face was drained of color.

"What's wrong?" I said.

She shook her head and shut the drawer. "I'm afraid I can't show you the file after all."

"Why not?"

"Because, Ms. McCone, it is not there. And from what I can tell, a large number of our other files have vanished as well."

I left Ann Bates rummaging through her file cabinets, trying to figure out exactly what was missing, and drove to Allen Keller's home. The maid who answered the door told me the doctor wasn't in, but refused to say where he had gone. On my way back to the MG, I checked the garage; there was no car inside, so it was a good bet the maid was telling the truth. I thought for a minute and then remembered his boat, the *Princess Jane*, at the marina next to the Sand Dollar. It was worth a try. I drove over there and spotted the cruiser tied up at the far end of an outer slip. The location was reasonably private and the cruiser, which had to be at least thirty feet, was luxurious. I understood why Keller and Jane had chosen to meet there.

The marina was almost deserted on this weekday morning. As I walked out toward Keller's slip, all I heard were the cries of gulls and the creaks of the mooring hawsers. Then I heard another sound—the clink of a bottle against a glass.

Keller sat on a folding chair on the afterdeck of the

cruiser. He wore cutoff jeans and no shirt, and his stomach sagged over his belt. When I came alongside the boat, he was setting a gin bottle down on the table next to him. He looked up at me, squinting and shading his eyes from the sun, then said, "Go away."

I stepped on board anyway.

"You do as you please, don't you?" He picked up his glass and drank off half the clear liquid.

"Most of the time." I looked around and found another folding chair. Keller watched me set it up.

"I could throw you off of here." But his words held no menace.

"You could, but you look like you might need some company."

He shrugged. I sat down in the chair.

"How'd you know I was here?" he asked.

"I guessed, since this was where you and Jane used to go."

He paused, glass halfway to his lips. "Somebody's been talking. Who?"

"Nobody you know."

"Not Ann Bates. She wouldn't."

"No, not Ann. Let's just say I heard some gossip."

"Yeah, sure. Everybody's heard the gossip." He drank, then added, "If you're going to stay, at least have a drink."

If that was what it would take to get him talking, I would. Besides, it was hot there in the sun. "I'll take a beer if you've got one."

"I think there are some in the fridge below."

"Do you want me to get it?"

"No." He stood up, went to the entrance to the cabin, and disappeared. In a minute or so he returned with a chilled Coors. He handed it to me and reached immediately for the gin bottle. From his speech and movements, Keller wasn't drunk yet, but at this rate he soon would be.

"So you heard the gossip and came to hold my hand." His expression was sardonic, mouth pulled down on one side.

"Her death was a bad shock, wasn't it?"

"You could say that."

"Why'd you lie to me about knowing her?"

"Why should I have gone into it? She wasn't really missing—I knew that, and you knew it too because you'd talked to her mother."

"You knew it because she was staying with you."

He shook his head. "No. She wasn't with me, at least not the whole week."

"Where was she?"

His eyes left mine and flicked toward the bow. "She was elsehwere."

"Where?"

"I don't know. It doesn't matter now."

"It may."

"No." He drank more gin. "Not now it doesn't."

"Why wasn't she with you?"

"She needed privacy to do her research, and she didn't want to involve me anyway."

"What research?"

He made a motion with his hand, as if trying to erase his words.

"What kind of research?"

"Forget it."

A telephone that sat on the deck next to the companionway door began ringing. Keller got up and answered it, standing with his back to me.

While he talked, I thought over my visit to his house. Keller probably was telling the truth about Jane not staying there, because he would not have admitted me so freely and let me stay so long if she were there or likely to return. But what about this "research?" What had she been—?

"I said, don't worry about it!" Keller's voice was suddenly loud. "They'll turn up. . . . No, I'm not coming in today. . . . I don't know when—For God's sake, Ann, just hold things together there. Is that too much to ask? I'll be in when I can." He slammed the receiver into its cradle and strode back to his chair, his face mottled with anger.

"Ann Bates," I said.

He glared at me. "You seem to know a great deal about my friends and associates."

"I know Ann because I just came from The Tidepools. She was calling about the missing files, wasn't she?"

He sighed and leaned forward, elbows on knees, head in hands. "The files are not missing, they've merely been misplaced. She's making a big deal out of nothing. Jesus, why did I get up today? What the fuck is happening to me? When did it all get so out of control?"

I waited, but he just sat there, staring down at the desk. My beer can was empty, and the ice in his glass had melted. I stood up and said, "You can use a fresh drink; I'll get some ice and another beer—"

He looked up quickly. "No, I'll do it." This time his steps were unsteady as he walked toward the companionway.

I waited until his head disappeared, then got up, and looked down there. I could see a small, compact galley, but that was all. I glanced down at the telephone at my feet and made a note of its number. By the time Keller returned, I was back in my deck chair.

"About that research of Jane's . . ." I opened my beer and took a swallow.

Keller's angry expression returned. "If you don't want to get pitched over the side, drop it. I don't even know why I'm letting you stay aboard."

But I could guess; Keller wasn't a man who could bear loneliness in the face of his loss. To prove it, he began to talk, his words slurring as they spilled out.

"But, then, I don't know anything anymore. How *do* you know when your life gets out of control? There was a time when I thought I had it all and now I can't even remember when that was. I was a doctor, a good doctor, and I was going to ease pain. I'd been to England, seen the work they were doing in the hospices there, and I'd inherited enough capital to start my own here. The Tidepools. Ease pain. Jesus."

"But you do good work there."

"Sure. Good work. And we take their money. Sometimes we even . . . Jesus." He poured a full glass of gin and began in on it. "You know, it probably got out of control up there when I brought Ann in. She had a lot of ideas about making a profit and they sounded good, but what they did was bastardize the original concept. But the reason I brought her in and went for those ideas was because it had gotten out of control with me first. You know what I mean?"

"Sort of."

"Cars. Country club. A house in the hills. This boat. The kind of women I chose. The things they wanted—Oriental carpets, sheets, towels, sterling silver. And each time one of them turned out that way, I'd choose another. Another with the same wants and needs. And me with mine, always looking to another woman for the solution. And then Janie."

"Was she different?"

"Yes. She was different. She was willing to work for it all. When everything went to hell and it looked like I was going to lose the house and the cars and maybe even The Tidepools, she didn't worry. She just went to San Francisco, said she'd find a way to buy us out of the trouble."

"With a social worker's salary?"

It was a mistake to have asked it. He frowned and set down his glass. "I'm talking too much. I always do when I drink. For that matter, I'm drinking too much. You'd better go."

"No, what you've said is very interesting. It's a real commentary on contemporary values—"

Keller stood up. "Like I said, you'd better go."

I went. But at the other end of the parking lot, I stopped at the marina office. It was locked, and a sign indicated someone would be back at one-thirty. That might help me, if my plan worked at all. There was a phone booth outside the office, and I stepped in there, dug out a dime, and called the number of the phone on Keller's boat. When he answered, I pitched my voice higher than usual and said, "Dr. Keller, this is Beth at the office."

"Who?"

"Beth. You probably don't know me; I'm new. Anyway, I wonder if you could come up here for a few minutes."

There was a sigh. "Why?"

"It's about those things the woman who was staying on your boat lost last week."

"What things?" His tone was suddenly more alert.

"Oh, didn't she tell you? She lost a key ring and a checkbook. One of the other slip holders turned them up. We have them here if you'd like to—"

"I'll be right there."

It had been a guess, but it had turned out to be right on target. Now I'd have to move fast. I ran across the graveled parking lot, back along the slips, and along one of the side floats. In a couple of minutes, Keller hurried along the dock toward the office. I waited until he was past, then sprinted for his slip and climbed on board the cruiser. As I'd hoped, he hadn't locked the door to the companionway. I went down there, almost slipping on the ladder.

The galley was straight ahead, but that didn't interest me. I went aft, where there were sleeping quarters. The teak-paneled cabin had two built-in bunks with a dresser between them. On the dresser was a small tan suitcase with the initials JMA. Irrelevantly, I wondered what Jane Anthony's middle name had been.

The case was full of cosmetics, underwear, jeans, and tops—all thrown in together. Fastidious Jane had never packed—or repacked—these things. I looked through them, found nothing unusual, then turned my attention to the rest of the cabin. One bunk was rumpled, its covers turned back. The other was smooth and on it sat a cardboard box. I went over and saw it was full of file folders.

As I reached for the box, I heard a thump on the deck above. I froze, listening. Footsteps went toward the companionway and down the ladder, and then Keller appeared, his back to me, heading for the galley.

He was back much sooner than I'd anticipated. Had he realized the call was a fake? Would he search the boat? I flattened against the wall of the cabin, wishing the box of folders was still within reach.

There was the sound of an icetray being emptied and then the crack of a seal, probably on a fresh bottle of gin. Keller's voice said wearily, "Let them keep the stuff. It's of no use to me. Or to Janie anymore." Next I heard breaking glass. "Jesus Christ," Keller said. There was a long silence and then he added, "You've had enough, fellow."

Keller's footsteps left the galley and I held my breath, hoping he would go up on deck and leave the boat without the files. The footsteps came on, however, toward the cabin. I got ready and, as he stepped through the door, rushed past him, heading for the ladder.

Keller whirled. "Hey!"

I banged my knee on one of the rungs but scrambled up.

"Come back here, dammit!" Keller was right below me, grabbing for my ankle. He got a good hold on it, and I fell to the deck, then started crawling for the rail when he let go. He lurched up the ladder and grabbed me by my hair, yanking me backward. I screamed. He bent my arm behind me and glowered down, breathing gin into my face.

"That call was one of your cute tricks, eh?"

I tried to wrench free, but he held me firmly.

"So you know Jane stayed here," he said. "So what?"

"The police will be interested."

"Not when they find there's no evidence of her presence. Who are they going to believe—you or me?"

I didn't want to debate our relative credibility. I struggled harder, but he pinned both my arms behind my back and dragged me to my feet.

"You're trespassing, you know," he said. "Why don't I call the police and let them handle you?"

"Why don't you? When they arrive we can discuss what the personnel files from The Tidepools are doing below."

"Why shouldn't they be there? I was going over them, working here because it's quieter than my office."

"Sure you were."

"Like I said, who are they going to believe?"

He was right; they were his files and the police would believe him, particularly when he got Ann Bates to back him up, as I was sure he could. Still, I decided to call his bluff. "So pick up the phone and call Lieutenant Barrow."

He was silent for a moment, breathing hard. Then he chuckled. "No, I've got better plans for you."

"Such as?"

He twisted my body sideways, and one of his arms went under my knees, the other around my shoulders. I pushed out at him with my freed hands, but he lifted me and stepped over to the rail.

"Don't say I didn't warn you," he said.

In seconds, I was flying through the air, and then I hit the water. I started to yell but closed my mouth just in time before I went under. The water was cold and oil-slicked. When I bobbed to the top, my hair was plastered to my face, and I had to part it to look up at the boat. Keller leaned on the rail, laughing uproariously.

"That'll teach you to be so goddamn nosy!"

"Fuck you!" It was one of the few times in my life I'd ever said that.

It only made Keller laugh harder.

I began to swim in the opposite direction, toward the main dock, Keller's laughter following me. I'd lost both shoes sometime during the struggle, but my skirt—the grown-up-person skirt I'd worn to impress Ann Bates—greatly impeded my progress. I wanted to appear dignified, but it was impossible while attempting the Australian crawl, fully clothed, in six feet of dirty water. I could still hear Keller's laughter when I hauled myself up on the dock and sloshed off toward my car.

I'll get even, I told myself. I *will* get even. By the time I'm through with this case Allen Keller won't be laughing at anything.

14

I called Lieutenant Barrow as soon as I got back to the motel and told him what I'd found out at the *Princess Jane*—omitting the part about my impromptu swim. He said they'd already talked to Keller—who had claimed not to know where Jane had been during the week before her death—but promised to go out and talk to him again. I said I would check with Barrow later, and then hung up and took a long, hot shower. By the time I'd finished dressing and drying my hair it was after four.

One thing was certain: I was never going to get a look at The Tidepools' files now. I sat down and considered the problem, then decided to approach it from another angle.

At the public library, I requested the microfilms for the week of Barbara Smith's death once again. I read through them slowly, looking for any facts I might have skipped over before, then checked her obituary. It listed a sister,

Mrs. Susan Tellenberg of Port San Marco, as one of the survivors. I looked her up in the directory, found a number and address, and called her. The phone rang ten times with no answer.

When I left the library it was nearly dusk. I wanted to go to Salmon Bay, to talk with both Mrs. Anthony and John Cala, but I decided to stop by the police station first and see what Barrow had gotten out of Allen Keller. The desk sergeant told me the lieutenant was out of the office but due back any minute. I waited on a bench in the lobby, watching uniformed cops and plainclothesmen come and go. What business there was that evening was strictly routine: a father picking up a lost child, a wife filing a missing person report on her husband, a tourist reporting a stolen camera. After an hour it became apparent that Barrow either had been delayed or wasn't coming back, so I left a message that I'd stop by again and went out to my car.

I drove north to Salmon Bay along the now-familiar coastal highway and parked in front of Sylvia Anthony's house. It was dark and closed up, just like last time. Maybe Jane's mother had gone to stay with friends or relatives.

I looked over at Cala's junk-cluttered yard and saw a porch light on. At least I would get to talk to the fisherman. I took my keys from the ignition, but before I could get out of the car, Cala came through his front door. He was pulling on a windbreaker as he hurried down the walk toward a beat-up pickup truck. As soon as he jumped in, the truck's lights flashed on and its engine roared. I started my own car as the truck pulled away.

Cala drove fast through the rutted lanes to the coastal highway, then headed south. The truck had a distinctive broken taillight and was easy to keep in sight. Once on the main road, I dropped back and let a small car ease in between us. I followed Cala into Port San Marco and through the tourist area to the lower part of town near the boarded-up amusement park. He left the truck at the curb by the public beach and went to stand on the seawall.

I stopped a few yards down the street and watched as Cala checked his watch. Beyond the seawall the ocean was placid, its waves barely disturbing the image that the newly risen moon reflected on it. Cala stood on the wall for a few minutes, as if admiring the scene, then stepped onto the beach.

Leaving the MG where it was, I strolled slowly down the sidewalk, scanning the beach for Cala's figure. There were no other pedestrians, and the area had a desolate, rundown feeling. It even seemed colder here than in the brightly lit tourist section to the north, and I couldn't help contrasting it with the kaleidoscope of color and sound and smells I'd known as a child, before the amusement park died.

Cala was walking diagonally across the wide beach, toward the water but also toward the high board fence of the park. The fence was posted with NO TRESPASSING signs and colorful posters proclaiming it the future site of the Port San Marco Performing Arts Center. Above the fence, on the far seaward side, the old roller coaster towered, its girders dark against the evening sky.

Cala continued across the sloping beach to where the

park was built up on pilings. As I watched from the seawall, Cala ducked down and disappeared among them.

I went along the seawall to the perimeter of the park, then crossed the beach, keeping in the shadows. When I reached the pilings, I slipped under there as Cala had and crept forward, searching for him. I spotted him finally, going up a set of steps that led into the park above. It was a well-hidden entrance that could be seen only from directly under the roller coaster—or from the water, if you happened to be out there in a boat. That was probably how Cala knew about it.

But what was he doing here at the deserted amusement park? He had left his house in a hurry and had waited on the seawall after checking his watch. Was he meeting someone? If so, who? And why here, of all places?

From the direction of the steps I heard a door close. Cala must be inside the park. I followed, my footsteps muffled on the damp sand, and looked up the steps. The door at their top had once been padlocked, but the hasp hung on splintered wood. Vandals must have been at work here, and just kids looking for a place to drink and neck. I climbed the steps and touched the door. It swung open quietly.

It took a moment for my eyes to become accustomed to the dark. Then I made out a wide expanse of boardwalk and the outlines of abandoned booths. They were mere shells, but their signs—the signs of my youth—remained: COTTON CANDY, CORN DOGS, THREE RING TOSSES FOR A QUARTER. . . . TEST YOUR STRENGTH, IMPRESS YOUR LADY FRIEND, WIN A GIANT PANDA.

I slipped inside, shutting the door behind me, and

stood pressed against the wall. A clammy, salt-tanged breeze was blowing up through the cracks in the boardwalk and nearby something that sounded like old newspaper rustled, but otherwise I heard nothing. Cala was nowhere in sight.

To my left were more booths and the merry-go-round with its domed top. It had been stripped of its horses and, without them, the top looked like a flying saucer hovering ten feet above the platform. To the right was the Penny Arcade, the Fun House, and the Tunnel of Love. I went off that way, since the overhang of the buildings provided greater cover.

The park was so silent that, had I not seen Cala go in there, I would not have believed there was another soul within miles. I looked into the Penny Arcade and saw nothing but empty space and a row of skee-ball alleys. The mouth of the Tunnel of Love gaped at me, and I went over and glanced down into the trench that had once held the boats. It was dry now, full of beer cans and other trash. Moving along, I mounted the steps to the Fun House.

As I entered, a sudden motion startled me. I shrank back, my heart pounding. Then I realized that what I had seen was myself, reflected over and over in ripply shards of glass. The mirror—the one that made you short and fat, tall and skinny—had been smashed but still hung on the wall. I stared into it, seeing my face distorted into exaggerated lines of alarm. Curbing my urge to giggle with relief, I went on through the little maze of now-empty rooms. Nothing here. Cala must have gone the other way, toward the merry-go-round.

I had just reentered the room with the mirror when things began to happen.

First there was a muffled grunt, and then a thump. I froze, listening, trying to place the origin of the noises. Then I heard the sound of running feet. I bounded out of the Fun House in time to see a dark figure come down the steps from the Tunnel of Love's boarding platform and sprint toward the door to the beach. It wasn't Cala; the person was too short and much thinner.

The figure saw me and whirled, then darted to the side as I ran toward it. Suddenly there was a rumbling sound. A three-foot-high boxy shape came at me and caught me squarely in the stomach. I fell forward over it, and it continued rolling, slamming me against the counter of the cotton candy booth. Pain exploded in the small of my back. I slid off the thing that had hit me and fell to the ground.

I tried to get up, but I was pinned between the bulky object and the booth. As I flailed around, the door to the beach slammed and I heard footsteps run down the stairs.

I kicked out and freed myself. The clumsy object was one of those chairs on wheels that porters used to roll along the boardwalk, charging patrons a small fee for the privilege of riding in old-fashioned style. Giving it a vicious shove, I got to my feet and ran to the door and down the steps. I couldn't see anyone among the dark pilings.

I ran through them and looked up the beach. There was no fleeing figure, no one scaling the seawall, no car roaring away from the curb. My MG and Cala's truck were still parked where we had left them. Whoever had fled must have run south down the beach. I scurried through the pilings and peered into the darkness. In the distance, I thought I could make out a shape, but just barely. There was no possibility of overtaking him now.

But what about Cala? His truck was here, which meant he must still be inside the park. I climbed the steps again, rubbing my back where it hurt, and looked around. It was as quiet in there as before. I waited in the darkness for a minute, then took out my small flashlight and went toward the Tunnel of Love.

I shone the flash around the mouth of the tunnel, then went up the steps to the platform where you boarded the boats. The tunnel curved away into darkness—the only way to explore the place would be to climb down into the trench. I turned the flash downward. It picked out old newspapers, cans, and bottles. Some of the newspapers were splashed with a dark red liquid.

I stiffened, then moved the flash a couple of feet. There was more red, and a foot in a tennis shoe.

Slowly I moved the flash again, up a leg to the torso and finally to the face of John Cala. He lay on his back in the trench. The front of his windbreaker was soaked with blood. It had to be a stabbing, since I hadn't heard a shot; and the knife had apparently hit an artery, because the blood had spurted all over.

I stepped back and almost tumbled down the steps from the platform. Grasping the railing, I leaned against it, closing my eyes and forcing down the bile rising in my throat.

Blood. So much blood. Not a clean killing, like Jane

Anthony. A messy killing. Blood. A sickly-sweet smell. And the rising stench of feces . . .

My stomach lurched and I ran down the steps, fell to my knees, and retched. I hadn't eaten or drunk anything since the two beers on Keller's boat that morning, so what I ended up with was a fine case of the dry heaves. After a minute they stopped and I felt around for where I'd dropped the flashlight.

My fingers encountered it and I shone its beam around me. There had once been public phone booths in the park and I wondered if they were still in working order. I had to call the police, had to get them out here, had to explain . . .

Explain what? Explain why I was the one who found all the corpses in Port San Marco? How was this going to look? What if, in the course of questioning me, Barrow asked to talk to my client? If he found out I didn't even have one . . .

Well, that couldn't be helped. All I could do right now was find a phone booth. There didn't seem to be any in the park and, in a way, that relieved me. I'd just as soon get out of here. When I reached the stairs to the beach, I gave the Tunnel of Love a final glance. Its mouth yawned at me, like the door of a crypt.

15

Music poured from Don Del Boccio's apartment as he came out and looked over the bannister at me. It sounded like Tchaikovsky—great, surging crescendoes. I stood, my hand on the railing, looking up.

Don wore a forest green terrycloth bathrobe and a huge grin. His black hair was tousled and fell onto his forehead. "Now, this time it's sure to be a social call!"

"I hope it's all right to drop in this late." I remained where I was, still clutching the railing. "I got your message at the motel and I...I need someone to talk to."

His bushy brows drew together in an expression of concern. "Sure. Come on up."

I climbed the stairs, feeling terribly weary. When I got to the top, Don's eyes searched my face and then he ushered me in. He motioned for me to sit on the blue rug and went to the stereo. "Let me turn this down." I dropped to the floor.

The music sank several decibels and then Don came over and sat in front of me. "What's wrong?"

"I stumbled onto another murder." Quickly I told him about John Cala.

Don was silent for a moment. "John. My God. Didn't the police suspect him of having something to do with Janie's death?"

"Apparently he found her body before I did."

"And now someone's killed him."

"In the same way, and in the same kind of deserted place. Did you know Cala?"

He nodded. "Everybody from Salmon Bay knows everybody else. John was kind of a troublemaker, and not very bright. He dropped out of school in tenth grade and went into his father's fishing business. I guess he did all right."

"Really? He lived in a little house with a dreadful assortment of junk in the front yard."

"That doesn't mean much; it's the way his family lived. In Salmon Bay, nothing ever changes from generation to generation."

"I guess not. Did he have a family?"

"No. He married twice, that I heard of. The first wife was killed in an auto accident, the second left him. Claimed he beat her."

"Do you think he did?"

"Maybe. I know he was a confirmed male chauvinist; goes with the territory, I guess."

I sighed. "It really doesn't matter now. He's dead.

And his murderer escaped. And the police think somehow it's all my fault."

Don's eyes widened. "They don't suspect *you*?"

"Oh, no. They just think I bungled everything. If I hadn't found Cala, his body might have lain there until demolition on the amusement park started next spring. But do they appreciate that fact? No, because I'm a private operative, I bungled it. I suppose if a real cop had followed him there and found his body, they'd have given *him* a medal." My voice broke, from weariness and frustration, and Don took my hand.

"Why don't you let it go for now?" he said softly.

"How can I?"

"Relax. Have some wine."

"That sounds good."

He stood up. "How about some food?"

My stomach still felt uneasy. "No."

"Yes."

"Please, no."

"You need to eat. A little salami, some cheese. It's good for you."

"Mother Del Boccio."

"Humor me. I'm Italian."

"What does that have to do with it?"

"Everything."

He went to the kitchen and quickly produced red wine, cheese, crackers, a dish of black olives, and a foot-long salami.

"You're always feeding me," I said.

"I know." He sat back down and gestured at the food. "Eat."

Surprisingly, I was able to get down a respectable amount. It did make me feel better, but didn't relax me enough to get my mind off Cala's murder.

"If only I knew why he went out on that pier," I said. "And why he went to the amusement park. I know he was meeting someone there. But who?"

Don smiled, leaning back against a pillow. "Full of questions, aren't you?"

"It's my stock in trade. Somehow, I've always known the right questions to ask. And people open up to me. I'm a complete stranger, but they'll still tell me things they wouldn't tell their best friend."

"You have an open face. You look like you won't judge people." Don's eyes moved over my face, in the same appreciative but inoffensive way they'd appraised my body when he first saw me. I smiled back and lay down, my head on a pillow, feeling warm and finally relaxed. The wine had made me drowsy and a little disconnected from my surroundings.

"I've always asked too many questions," I said, aware I was almost repeating myself. "My mother used to get mad at me. 'Why, why, why?' she used to say. '*Why* are you always asking why?' "

Don chuckled and got up. He turned off the lights, brought a candle from the kitchen, lit it, and set it on the rug. Then he lay down, his elbow on the pillow next to me, head propped on his hand.

"Tell me about you," he said. "You asked me the right questions earlier this week and I gave you my life history. Now it's your turn."

"There's not a whole lot to tell. I'm from San Diego,

got a sociology degree from Berkeley, couldn't find a job. I'd done security work part-time while I was going to school, so I went back into that and got training as a detective."

"And your family—what are they like?"

"An average middle-class clan."

He traced one finger along my hairline. "I find it hard to believe that an average middle-class clan produced someone like you."

"Hmmm. Well, I guess you're right. Now that I think of it, I'm the most normal of the lot."

"Tell me about them."

I shut my eyes, visualizing my parents' old rambling house in San Diego and all the people who had lived there at one time or another. "I have two older brothers. One's married with two kids, the other's single. They get in trouble with the law a lot."

"The kids or your brothers?"

"My brothers. The kids are too young yet."

"What do they do?"

"Minor things. Overdue traffic tickets. Getting rowdy in bars. My brother John once punched out a cop. Then I have two younger sisters."

"Do they beat up on cops?"

"No. Their specialty is pregnancy."

"Oh."

"One of them lives on a farm near Ukiah. She has three kids, each by a different boyfriend. My other sister lives in a suburb of L.A. She's got four kids and is married to a musician."

"Are all the kids his?"

"Oh, yes. Unlike Patsy, Charlene is very monogamous. That's the problem."

"Problem?"

I opened my eyes. Don had a bemused smile on his lips and the candlelight flickered over his tanned, handsome face. "Charlene's husband keeps leaving her. Not for anything like other women—just to go on tour with this country-western band. He'll go off for six, eight months at a time and then, when he shows up, bingo! She's pregnant again."

"It sounds serious."

"Oh, it is. They've only been married five years. God knows how many kids they'll end up with."

"What about you?" Don ran his finger down my cheek and along my jawbone. "Do you want kids?"

"I never think about them. Good Lord—I don't even know if I want to get married."

"And I'll bet your mother worries about that."

"Oh, yes. That, and the fact I'm always getting mixed up in murders. My poor parents! All they ever wanted were good Catholic kids—and look what they got."

"How do they handle it?"

"Well, my mother's an expert at coping. She holds the family together through the worst trials and traumas."

"And your dad?"

"When we were younger, he wasn't around all the time. He was a chief petty officer in the navy and managed to pull a fair amount of sea duty. Now he's retired and works as a cabinetmaker. When things get to be too much for him, he just goes off to his workshop in the garage and plays his guitar."

"What? Another musician?" Don's finger stopped moving along my chin and he stared down at me.

I grinned. I loved to tell people about my eccentric family. "Only amateur."

"What does he play? Rock?"

"No. Irish folk ballads."

"I thought McCone was a Scottish name."

"Scotch-Irish."

"But you look Indian."

"Shoshone. One-eighth."

"Ye gods." He brushed a tendril of hair away from my face and wound a thick lock of it through his fingers. "Did you know your family was, uh . . . not usual when you were growing up?"

"Oh, no. For years, I thought we were just like everybody else. It wasn't until high school that I became aware of certain . . . oddities."

"What enlightened you?"

"It's a long story."

"We have all night."

"Yes, we do, don't we?"

Don and I exchanged solemn looks for a moment. Then I said, "Well, I really figured it out because of our Corvair. You know, one of those little compact cars with the engine in the rear?"

Don nodded.

"One day, in tenth grade, I was telling a girlfriend about it. You see, there was so much junk in our garage—my father's guitar included—that we couldn't drive the car in all the way. During the winter, its rear end stuck out and the engine got cold and wouldn't start."

"All right. So far I can picture it."

"Every night," I went on, "when it was time to go to bed, my dad would take this torchlight out to the car. He'd plug it in and turn it on, and then he'd open the rear hood and stick the light in there to keep the engine warm. And then he'd take a couple of old quilts and tuck the back of the car in for the night."

Don opened his mouth, but I held up my hand. "I know what you're going to say. Just what my friend in high school did. There I was, telling her this story about how clever my dad was to keep the car's engine warm in spite of everything, and she said . . ." I started to laugh. "She said, as logical as could be, 'Why doesn't he just back the car into the garage?' "

Don started to laugh too, and then I laughed harder, and he laughed harder still. He buried his face against my neck and put his arms around me and we laughed and laughed. Finally we lay there, holding each other, panting and bursting into occasional giggles. After a few minutes, Don raised his face, looked down into mine, and kissed me.

What with the wine and the weariness, I almost felt I was floating. I kissed him back, aware of nothing but his lips and the soft fabric of his robe. And then I felt the rough-but-gentle touch of his hands on my body. And responded, my own hands on him.

Soon my clothes and his robe lay heaped on the floor next to us, and we merged together in slow but powerful motion on the blue rug. And the aftermath of its climax brought shared peace and a shield from the haunting shadow of violent death.

Sometime during the night we moved to the bed in the alcove and slept, close in each other's arms. And, toward morning, I awoke with a start from dreams of Corvairs wrapped in blood-spattered quilts. Awoke thinking of one thing that might have made John Cala go out to the old pier.

A car. The presence of a car he'd thought he recognized.

16

The morning sunlight shining on the water at Salmon Bay had that pale quality I associated with autumn, and there was a slight chill in the air. I parked my car by the side of the main road and contemplated Rose's Crab Shack.

An hour earlier, after calling Barbara Smith's sister and still getting no answer, I'd allowed Don to feed me a disgraceful amount of scrambled eggs, sausage, hash browns, and toast. But I supposed a cup of coffee wouldn't hurt me, and here at the Crab Shack it might open the door to a conversation about the night that Jane Anthony died. I got out of the car, crossed the road, and went into the hole-in-the-wall restaurant.

There were several people in there—the same white-haired old man behind the counter, two men in fishing clothes, and a woman with a little girl of about ten. I started to sit down at the counter, but the old man rose and said, "What are you doing here?"

The room grew very still.

"I thought I'd have a cup of coffee," I said.

"Not in here, you won't."

"Why not?"

The old man came around the counter and stopped within two feet of me. He was my height and frail, but with his hands on his hips and his white-stubbled chin jutting out, he was forbidding enough to keep me from sitting down. He merely stood there, glaring at me with watery blue eyes.

"Why not?" I repeated.

"We don't want your kind in here."

"My kind?"

"Troublemakers. That's what you've brought us—trouble."

"How did I do that?" I was aware of everyone else in the room watching us.

The old man reached for a folded newspaper lying on the counter and shook it at me. "It's all in here. First Miz Anthony's girl, and now John Cala."

"I only found them, you know. I didn't kill them."

"That's what *you* say."

"Look, I'm trying to help the police find out who did it. I came in here to ask you if you'd seen any cars going out to the old pier the night Jane died."

He took a step closer. "I was in here behind the counter the whole time. You ought to know that."

I backed up, looking around. "Well, what about everybody else? Did any of you see a car that night?"

They were all silent. The little girl put her hand to her mouth.

The old man kept coming and I kept backing up. He held the newspaper rolled in his hand, as if he were about to discipline a puppy.

"Come on," I said, "somebody must have seen something."

"That's what the cops said. And I told them the same thing. Nobody saw nothing." We had reached the entrance now, and the old man held the screen door open.

"Don't you care if the killer's caught?" I asked.

He motioned impatiently, shooing me outside. "All we want is to be left alone, lady. That's all anybody here wants." He slammed the door and hooked it shut.

I stood there peering through the screen at him and frowning. "What are you afraid of?"

The old eyes shifted. "Nobody here's afraid of nothing."

"Are you afraid one of you might have done it? Is that it—you think somebody who lives here in the village is the killer?"

He started to turn.

"Look at it this way," I said. "Do you really want to live with a killer on the loose among you?"

In a flash, he had the screen door open and was outside, coming at me. "Get out of here!" He waved the paper in the air, then took aim at my behind. I ran just like a puppy would.

At my car I stopped and looked back. The old man stood in front of the Crab Shack, glaring at me. The other customers had come outside and were watching in silent amazement. The scene suddenly seemed funny to me, and I chuckled ruefully as I got into my car and continued down the road. Once out of sight of the restaurant, I parked again and began canvassing on foot.

At the first house an old woman in a striped housedress told me she hadn't seen anything. She minded her own business, she said, and didn't see why others couldn't do the same.

At the second house a younger woman with a baby on her hip said she didn't have time to pay attention to what went on outside her own yard. Besides, if this was a come-on to get her to buy something, I could forget it. Her husband had lost his job at the supermarket, and they were collecting unemployment.

No one was home at the next house, and the one after that had two German shepherds in the yard. They barked and jumped on the fence and looked at me hungrily. I decided to bypass that one.

Crossing the street, I found an old man working in his garden. No, he said, he hadn't noticed anything, but had I ever seen such beautiful marigolds as his?

Truthfully I said I hadn't.

The old man plucked one and gave it to me. I slipped it through the buttonhole of my jacket and went on.

The neighboring house was vacant. At the next a woman shouted from behind a closed door for me to go away. Two little boys playing in the yard of the last house said their mother wasn't home.

I went into the general store and was told to get out unless I was buying something. Finally I reached the Shorebird Bar and went inside.

It was dark, with a long scarred bar and a fly-specked

mirror that reminded me of the Remedy Lounge back home. The bartender's apron was cleaner, however, and the glasses looked like somebody had taken care in washing them. There were two customers, men at the far end who were shaking dice. I sat down a few stools away from them and ordered a beer. The bartender looked as though he wanted to refuse to serve me, then shrugged and went to get it. When he came back, I asked him about the night of Jane's death.

He frowned, polishing the bar with a rag. "That was a busy night. Of course, they all are. Ain't much else to do here but drink. I don't recall anything unusual, until I heard the sirens."

"Do many people drive out that way?"

"No. Isn't much reason to. The police asked me the same question, and I couldn't tell them anything either." Then he looked at me with suspicion. "Why're *you* asking?"

"I'm working with the police."

"Yeah? Who?"

"Lieutenant Barrow."

Apparently he knew and liked Barrow, for he nodded and called down the bar to the two customers, "Hey, fellows, you remember the night Miz Anthony's girl got killed?"

They stopped rolling the dice and turned to look at us. They were both bald, one fat and the other skinny, probably in their fifties. The skinny one said, "I sure do, and it's a damned shame."

"This lady here is trying to find out who done it."

They hesitated, exchanging looks.

"She's okay," the barkeep said. "She's helping out a friend of mine on the cops."

"The cops can use all the help they can get," the skinny one said.

"Even from a lady," the other added.

I said, "Were either of you here that night?"

The fat one grinned slyly. "We're always here. You could call us regulars."

"I'm trying to find out if anyone saw a car driving out to the old pier. It would have been a half hour, maybe an hour before you heard the police sirens."

They both frowned. Then the fat one nodded. "There was a car, but I'm not sure how long before the sirens."

"What kind of a car, do you remember?"

"It was a foreign job. I noted it because we don't get too many around here."

"Do you recall what kind?"

"I couldn't put a name to it. It was what you call a sports car. Red. In pretty bad shape. Engine sounded like it had a cough."

The stirrings of excitement I'd been feeling disappeared. The wonderful machine he had just described was mine.

"Does that help you any?" the fat man asked.

"Some. Did you see any cars before that one?"

He shook his head. "I was just getting here. You want, we could ask some of the other boys."

"Do that. Thanks." I stood up. "I'll stop by again later."

The bartender nodded and went back to polishing the scarred surface in front of him. The "boys" went back to their dice.

I left and stood outside, looking off toward the pier. My morning's efforts seemed fruitless and now I wondered why I had even bothered. The police would have canvassed the village thoroughly—and, given their official status, at least would not have been ingloriously chased out of the Crab Shack. I had better get back to town and try Barbara Smith's sister once again.

"Lady?" The voice came from behind me.

I turned. It was the little girl who had been in the Crab Shack with her mother. She was dressed in jeans and a blue T-shirt, and had bare feet. Her blond hair was pulled up in a ponytail and secured with a pink plastic barette.

"Hi," I said. "What's your name?"

"Rachel."

"That's a nice name. Where's your mom?"

She motioned at the store down the street. "Getting the groceries. I'm not supposed to talk to you."

"Why not?"

"They say you're an outsider. We don't like outsiders here."

Lord, they taught them young! "Who doesn't?"

She paused, looking down and running her bare toes through the dust. "My mom. And my dad. Most everybody."

"What about you?"

She looked up, fixing solemn eyes on my face. "I don't mind strangers. At least I don't mind you. And I like your car."

"You do, huh?"

"Yes. Could I sit in it, do you think?"

"Won't that make your mom mad?"

She glanced at the store. "She'll be in there a long time. She has a big list. Can't I sit in your car? Please!"

"Okay," I said. "Come on."

We went down the road and I held the passenger door open for her. Rachel hopped in and began to examine the dashboard. I remained standing beside the car; I was not going to get myself accused of child-stealing.

"Does this radio work?" Rachel asked.

"Yes. Do you want to hear it?"

"Please."

I reached in and put my key in the ignition, then flicked the radio on. A disc jockey's voice filled the air, going on about the fifties sock hop to be held at Port San Marco High on Saturday. His style was not nearly so frantic as Don's. Don. Thinking of him gave me a momentary rush of pleasure.

"The radio in my dad's car is busted," Rachel said. "It has been for years."

I turned my attention back to the little girl. "Is that so?"

"Yes." She turned, her forearms resting on the window, and looked up at me. "The real reason I wanted to sit in the car is to talk about what you were asking back there." She jerked her head in the direction of the Crab Shack.

I'd suspected she had more on her mind than the MG. "Oh?"

"About the cars the night the lady was killed. I'm not supposed to know about the lady being killed, but I do. And I saw something."

"Tell me."

She looked around. "I can't."

"Why not?"

"My mom said not to. She said to forget it so we wouldn't get involved. You're never supposed to get involved."

I squatted down beside the car. "Rachel, your mom is right. Sometimes getting involved is a bad thing. But there are other times when it's important. Times when you can help other people."

"Like you?"

"Like me."

She considered this solemnly. "Knowing about the car will help you?"

"Yes."

"A lot?"

"A whole lot."

She nodded as if she'd already known that. Then she said, "There's this Garfield doll at the store. I've been saving up for it, and I've almost got enough. But I need two more dollars."

It surprised me so much that my mouth dropped open.

"Only two dollars," Rachel repeated.

"Did you parents also teach you that tactic?" I muttered.

"What?"

"Nothing." I dug in my bag and held up the money. "I give you two dollars, you tell me about the car, right?"

"Right." She reached for it.

I pulled it back; I didn't like the idea of bribing a child. But then, she'd proposed it. "Tell me first."

Her lower lip pushed out. "How do I know you'll pay me if I tell first?"

Rachel had been watching too much TV, I decided. "Don't worry. I'll pay."

"All right." She leaned forward through the window, her small face conspiratorial. "That night I was playing in the front yard of our house." She motioned down the road. "I wasn't supposed to be out there; my mom thought I was in my room. But I like it outside when it's dark."

I glanced back at the store. Rachel's mother was nowhere in sight, but I was worried she would come out at any moment. "What did you see, Rachel?"

She pouted again.

I held up the two dollar bills.

"I saw a car go out there. It parked and then its lights shut off."

"What kind of car?"

"Like my dad's. That's why I noticed it."

"What kind of car does he have?"

"A VW. A dark blue one."

"And this was a VW?"

"Yes. A blue one, just like Dad's."

"What happened then?"

"My mom came out and called me. And I went inside."

It *would* be a VW, one of the most common cars on the California highways. Still, it was a lead. I held out the two dollars to Rachel. Her small hand closed over them quickly and she stuffed them in her pocket. I stood up and opened the car door for her.

"Maybe you'd better not tell your mother we talked," I said.

"I never tell her anything I don't have to." She jumped out of the car and started off toward the store. "Thanks, lady!" she called over her shoulder.

What a polite little extortionist! Was it the parents' fault? I wondered. Television? Something in the water? And what about people like me, who bribed children?

I decided I'd better leave philosophical considerations for another day, and headed back toward Port San Marco.

17

I went to the Mission Inn to phone Barbara Smith's sister, Susan Tellenberg, and check for messages. There was one—from Abe Snelling, of all people. Perhaps the photographer wanted to rehire me. I depressed the receiver and direct-dialed his home in San Francisco. He answered immediately.

"Thanks for calling," he said. "Hank Zahn told me where you were. It was in the papers about you finding that dead man. He was the one they originally suspected of killing Jane, wasn't he?"

"Yes."

"You think he did do it?"

"No. I think he knew who did, and that got him killed."

There was a long silence. When Snelling spoke, his voice was flat. "So they aren't any closer to finding the person now than before."

"Not really."

"Has anything else come up about Jane?"

"What do you mean?"

"Well, anything that might . . . I don't know. That might explain why she was murdered."

I had the impression that Snelling had something specific in mind but didn't want to say. "Well, I did find out where she was that week. She has a boyfriend down here and she was staying on his boat doing research."

"Research?" Now he sounded astonished.

"Not of a scholarly sort. I think Jane was looking into an old murder that happened at the place where she used to work, a hospice called The Tidepools. She was going through their personnel files—the boyfriend, Allen Keller, is part owner there and probably brought them to her at the boat."

"Why on earth was she doing that?"

"She must have had an idea who the killer was and wanted to verify it with the records."

"But why?"

I hesitated. Snelling had been Jane's friend and might not like what I was about to say. But, then, by his own admission they hadn't been all that close. "I think she intended to blackmail the killer. The boyfriend here is in bad financial shape and she may have been trying to help him out. In fact, she went to San Francisco originally with the idea of making money to buy him out of his trouble."

Again Snelling surprised me with his reaction. He said

in a matter-of-fact tone, "You mean she came here looking for this killer."

"Or a lead to him."

"Amazing." But he didn't sound amazed at all. Of course, Snelling struck me as a good judge of character, and this new information may have fit in with what he had already guessed about Jane.

"Do you want to reopen the case?" I asked.

He ignored the question. "Did the police look over those personnel records?"

"I doubt they've had the chance. Keller was aware I knew they were on the boat, so he would have returned them to The Tidepools right away. The police would have to subpoena them, and I don't think there's been time for that."

"I see."

"Abe, don't you want me to—"

"No. Jane's dead, and it's a waste of money anyway. I have to go now. I was working in the darkroom and I only answered the phone because I thought it might be you. Thanks for calling." Abruptly he hung up.

I sat staring at the receiver. Snelling had certainly gotten a lot of information for free. "Cheapskate," I muttered.

After a few seconds I called Susan Tellenberg's number. This time she answered and, when I asked if I could come talk to her about her sister, she sounded surprised but agreed. She gave me instructions on how to get there and said she'd see me within the hour.

* * *

The Tellenberg home was in the older section of the city, not far from Don's apartment house. It was a white frame cottage on a double lot, most of which was apple orchard. I went up to the door and was greeted by a plump blond boy of about five.

"Mama said you should come to the orchard," he told me, and took off across the front yard and through the trees. I followed, savoring the pungent aroma of overripe fruit. It reminded me of cider and football games and long walks home afterward, holding the hand of the cutest boy on the team. Funny how a new romance could beget memories of an old one. . . .

A woman with dark, curly hair and a rosy complexion sat cross-legged under the trees, tossing apples into a bushel basket. The little boy made a beeline for her and burrowed into her lap. She hugged him, adjusted the halter top he had knocked askew, and waved at me. I went over there.

"I'm Susan Tellenberg," she said, "and this is my son, Robbie."

The little boy wriggled out of her lap, gave me a military salute, and began to prance around, smashing apples. His mother gave him a stern look and he stopped. "Ms. McCone and I have things to talk about, Robbie. Perhaps you'd like to go in the house and find a book."

"I've read all my books."

"Reread one. You like the story about the rhinoceros."

"Rhinoceros!" His eyes grew wide and he turned and ran toward the house.

"He's young to be reading," I said.

"You're never too young." She grinned. "Besides, it keeps him occupied and it's cheaper than buying a TV. I hope you don't mind if we talk out here. I've got to get these windfalls picked up before they rot and disease the trees."

"No problem." I dropped to the ground, glad I'd worn jeans. "Let me help you."

"You want to know about Barbara," she said.

I picked up a couple of apples and tossed them into the basket. "Yes. I've read up on the case, in connection with another investigation, and I wanted to get an account of what happened from someone who really knew her."

"Is this other case something to do with Andy? Are you trying to find him?"

"Her husband? No. It's related to one of the people who used to work at The Tidepools."

"Good." She nodded with satisfaction and moved over to another pile of windfall apples.

I moved too. "Why good?"

"Because Andy didn't kill my sister, and I don't want him found. By now he's started a new life and he's entitled to it."

"It sounds as if you like him."

"I like Andy a lot. He put up with plenty from my sister and, on top of that, to be suspected of murdering her... Well, it's too unfair. I only wish he hadn't run; there was no need to."

"Oh?"

She must have interpreted the comment as skeptical, because her eyes flashed. "Barbara's death was a suicide. Andy ran because the police started raising all kinds of stupid speculation."

"He must have been very frightened."

She shrugged. "Andy always was a bit of a coward. But a nice coward, a gentle man. He wouldn't hurt anyone, least of all Barbara. He loved her, for some reason."

"Tell me about Barbara."

Susan relaxed, now that we were off the subject of Andy. "It may sound as if I disliked my sister. That isn't really true. It was just that she had so many problems—in addition to the cancer, I mean—and they were all ones she brought on herself."

"Such as?"

"She drank too much, took all sorts of pills. She'd been in and out of therapy for years, but never stayed long enough for it to do her any good."

"Did they ever diagnose a specific mental illness?"

"She was a manic-depressive, and as she got older the mood swings became more and more severe. When she found out she had cancer, she went into the depressive state and stayed there. We—Andy and I—felt The Tidepools was the only way to keep her from killing herself. Others in the family—if you've read the newspaper accounts, those are the ones the reporters talked to afterward—didn't agree. Maybe they thought her manic phase was the real Barbara. At any rate, they resented Andy for convincing her to go to the hospice. And when the police began to suspect him, they didn't help one bit, with their talk of how she would never take her own life."

Susan Tellenberg had a lot of pent-up anger in her, and

I gathered she'd been fonder of Andy than a sister-in-law should be. I glanced at her left hand—no wedding ring. She could be widowed or divorced, with a crush on her sister's gentle husband.

I said, "But Andy convinced her to go to The Tidepools."

She nodded. "She didn't want to go, but he insisted. It was the one time during their entire life together that he got his way. Usually he'd knuckle under to her demands. I'd ask him why—it wasn't helping her get any better or take responsibility for her life—and he'd just say it was preferable to living in perpetual conflict. Anyway, Barbara went to The Tidepools, but she hated it from day one and made sure everybody knew that. And then she died. She must have saved up her medication, like the others did."

"The newspaper stories say she wasn't receiving it long enough to have saved it."

Susan shrugged and moved again with her basket. "Barbara might even have brought the drugs with her. Like I said, she was always taking one kind of pill or another."

"Did the autopsy show that what she took was the same as what they gave out at the hospice?"

"Apparently they couldn't be that specific. What they use there is a mixture, and an autopsy can't show exact proportions or brand names, just the types of drugs present."

That was true, and it widened the range of possible suspects. Anyone with access to common prescription drugs could have killed Barbara. "What exactly made Andy run?"

"I told you, the police suspected him."

"But there must have been some triggering factor."

Susan stopped picking up apples and looked into the branches of the tree above. Sunlight cast dappled shadows over her troubled face. She sat that way for a few moments, then said, "It was all the confusion over the money that did it."

"The money Barbara had inherited, you mean?"

"Yes. The police found out that Andy had drawn it all out of the bank in cash a few days before Barbara died."

"Why did he do that, do you know?"

She shook her head.

"Didn't he ever talk to you about it?"

"No." She looked up into the trees again. "By the time I heard about it, Andy was gone. I've thought and thought about it ever since, but I can't come up with any answer except..."

"Except?"

"Except that Barbara made him do it. She was always making him do things."

"But why? What would she have needed forty thousand dollars in cash for?"

Susan rubbed her hands together and went back to picking up the apples. "I have a theory that she planned to bribe someone at the hospice to help her escape."

"Escape? She wasn't being held against her will, was she?"

"Well, not exactly. But you've got to remember Barbara was not really too well wrapped toward the end. She was paranoid and... I don't know. That's my theory."

She seemed to have a number of theories, all of them

conflicting and aimed at proving Andy didn't kill her sister. I sat there, rolling an apple between my palms.

Susan must have sensed my doubtfulness. "Look," she said, "I really don't know what Barbara intended. I never was able to understand what went on in her head. She had everything—she was smart and pretty and had a husband who loved her. She didn't have to work as a waitress and bring up a kid alone like I do. She didn't have a husband who abandoned her before the kid was even born, like I did. And, when it was time for our rich aunt to will her money to somebody, she chose Barbara, not me. But did Barbara appreciate any of that? No. Not my sister. All her life she worked so hard, so goddamned hard, at screwing up."

I remained silent, rolling the apple around and forming a theory of my own. "Had your sister accepted the fact she was going to die?"

"She believed it, if that's what you mean."

"But acceptance—the kind they talk about at The Tidepools—did she feel that?"

"Did she want to live out her life with dignity? Do something positive with what remained? I doubt it."

"Then how about this?" I pitched the apple into the basket. "How about if she did make Andy withdraw the money, so she could use it as a bribe—"

"That's what I said."

"But not a bribe to get out of the place. A bribe for someone to get her the drugs and administer them. What if she bought herself a mercy killing?"

Susan looked startled, but then nodded. "That's very

possible. It would explain why they didn't find the money with her things at the hospice."

"Of course," I went on, "why would she spend forty thousand dollars when she could have asked her own husband to help her?"

"No. Andy would never go along with something like that. He would never have helped her kill herself, and he certainly would never have gotten her the money had he known what it was for. She must have made up some story to tell him."

"Andy worked at Port San Marco General Hospital. He would have had access to drugs."

Stubbornly she shook her head. "No, he didn't. He was in the education department; it's a teaching hospital. He had nothing to do with drugs."

"I thought he was a medical technician."

"Yes, but he didn't handle drugs. He was a medical photographer. He took pictures of autopsies and put together slide shows and teaching aids for the hospital's educational programs."

I stared at her.

"He was a damned good photographer too. He used to exhibit the portraits he took as a hobby in shows around the area."

I sat in silence for several seconds, feeling a growing excitement. Things were beginning to fall into place at last.

"What's wrong?" Susan asked.

"Do you have a picture of Andy?"

"Yes, in the living room."

"Can I see it?"

She frowned, but stood up, brushing dead leaves off her jeans. "All right."

We went into the house, to an old-fashioned formal parlor. My hands were shaking as I took the framed portrait from Susan's hands. The face in it was bearded and the hair brown rather than blond, but it was the one I'd expected to see.

The younger, less careworn face of Abe Snelling.

18

I drove along the ridge above the Salinas Valley, ignoring the speed limit but keeping an eye out for the highway patrol. The air was hot and dry, and the needle on the MG's temperature gauge rose dangerously toward the red zone. Every few minutes I would check it, tell myself it would be fine, and then my eyes would drift back to it again. King City, I thought, I'll stop in King City. And try to phone Snelling again.

I'd called as soon as I left Susan Tellenberg's, planning to hang up if the photographer answered and then rush to San Francisco. But the phone had rung and rung, and finally I'd decided to risk making the trip anyway. After all, it might only mean Snelling was in the darkroom. Hadn't he said he unplugged the phone while working?

But, then, that might have been a lie—like all of Snelling's other lies. Because the night he'd claimed to have worked late in the darkroom—the night I'd kept calling to tell him of Jane's death—he most certainly had been in Port San Marco. Right now he might be hurrying for the airport or driving north, south, or east to a new identity.

My eyes strayed to the gauge. The needle had dropped slightly.

But why would Snelling run? He had no suspicion that I was close to uncovering his real identity. I hadn't told him I planned to see Susan Tellenberg. Because of my manner on the phone earlier, he probably felt more secure. Maybe he was in the darkroom right now, printing more of his wonderful photos.

The photos. That was another tragedy. While it seemed certain that Abe Snelling—or Andy Smith, whatever you wished to call him—was a killer, he also had a rare talent that would cease to be used when he was arrested. There would be no more of those portraits that probed to the core of their subjects' being, no more expressions of his unique understanding of human nature.

The needle on the temperature gauge rose again. Rapidly I calculated; it was only ten miles to King City.

Well, now I had answers to a number of my questions. I knew why Jane Anthony had gone to San Francisco, why Snelling had let her live at his house, why he had lied to me about how he met her. And I thought I knew why he had risked exposure by hiring me to find her.

I felt a certain responsibility for what had happened. Through me, Snelling had found out Jane was in the Port San Marco area. That had probably been enough to tell him how to locate her. He'd driven south, met her at the old pier, and . . .

The sign for the King City exit loomed up, and I moved into the right-hand lane.

What about John Cala? I was fairly sure he'd recognized Snelling leaving the pier, gone out there to see what he was doing, and found the body. Had he attempted to blackmail Snelling? I didn't think so. After all, Don had said Cala wasn't too bright. Probably Snelling had recognized him too and later lured him to the old amusement park with a promise of money. They were both from the area, and the boarded-up park was a likely place for a secret meeting at which cash was to change hands. But instead of cash . . .

I pulled off the freeway and turned into the gas station where I'd stopped earlier in the week. While the attendant filled my gas tank and radiator, I went to the phone booth and called Snelling. Again, the phone rang unanswered. I hurried to the car, paid with a credit card, and was soon back on the freeway.

Salinas slipped by. Gilroy. Morgan Hill. It was rush hour in San Jose. I fretted and cursed and my temperature rose, but at least the car's gauge remained constant.

I should have the radiator fixed, I thought. No, I should buy a new car. I had money in the bank, a fairly large reward from a grateful shipping company for whom I'd recovered a stolen consignment of cargo. It was more than enough for a new car. But then, it was almost enough for the down payment on a house. A house would solve the apartment problem. . . .

Now I was through San Jose and speeding up the freeway, where tract homes gave way to rolling hills and expensive estates. How many times had I driven this route in the past week? One, two, three, four. Lord, I was sick of the freeway!

One thing was certain: no one was going to be grateful and give me a reward for solving *this* case. No one was even paying me. So why was I doing this? Why was I rushing up here to face a dangerous man, putting myself in jeopardy? Why didn't I just call the police, tell them I'd located a fugitive, and let them handle it? I knew the number for San Francisco Homicide, had called it often in my year-and-a-half with Greg. I wouldn't have to talk to him; I knew most of the men on the squad. So why not pull off this endless freeway and make the call?

Was it because of the photos? Or because Susan Tellenberg had called Andy Smith a nice coward, a gentle man? Or was it because there were things that still *didn't* fit?

The last thirty miles went quickly. Route 280 rejoined 101 near the Daly City line, and soon I was exiting at Army Street and scaling the steep streets of Potrero Hill. It was after six; the demolition had stopped. The shells of houses stood dark and silent. So did the top story of Snelling's, but that didn't mean anything; the fence obscured the first floor. He could be there, or downstairs on the bedroom level.

I got my gun out of the glove box and stuck it in the outer compartment of my shoulder bag, where I could reach it quickly if I had to. Then I went up to Snelling's gate, keeping in the shadow of the fence.

The first thing I noticed was that the gate was open.

I paused, listening, then pushed it with my fingertips. It swung all the way back, revealing the overgrown yard.

No lights were on in the lower windows. I started down the path.

There was a rustling in the shrubbery to my left. I whirled, hand poised over my gun. A cat jumped lightly to the fence and down onto the other side. I relaxed, but only slightly, and kept going.

The front door was also open, the security chain hanging limp.

I stepped inside, waited until my eyes adjusted to the gloom, then went down the hall. The living room was dark, the draperies open. I could make out the photos on the wall, the chrome-and-leather furniture, the stairway to the top story. Everything seemed as it should be.

And then I noticed that the desk to the side of the fireplace had been ransacked. Its drawers were pulled out and their contents lay scattered on the desk itself, the chair in front of it, and the floor. A trail of papers led from there to the stairway. I listened, heard nothing, and decided to risk turning on a lamp.

Its soft glow filled the stark white room, and I could now see that books had also been removed from some shelves by the stairway. They were piled haphazardly on the floor, and a few were open, as if someone had been riffling through their pages. There was still no sound and, although I couldn't be sure, I felt the house was empty. Slowly I went to the stairway and climbed to the studio.

There was nothing there but the stool in the center. I glanced up at the skylights and saw a few wispy clouds highlighted against the early-evening sky. The door to the darkroom was wide open and, taking my gun out, I walked across the room.

It was pitch black. All I could hear was the bubbling of the print washer. I reached inside the door, found a light switch, and flicked it on. It was the switch for the safelight, and the room was bathed in its red glow. It illuminated the enlarger and the stainless steel tanks and the dryer and the light table. A couple of prints floated face down in the washer. There was nothing amiss here.

Or was there? I found another switch and flicked it, this time getting white light.

There was a strip of negatives in the enlarger's holder, and more of them, in protective plastic, spread out on the light table. In one corner, I spotted a file cabinet with its drawers open. Inside were folders full of prints, some of which had been emptied out onto the floor. Ransacked, just like downstairs.

But where on earth had Snelling been while this had been taking place?

I put my gun into my purse and, leaving the light on, went back downstairs to search the bottom floor. As I passed through the living room, something caught my eye—a crumpled piece of photographic paper, lying on top of a disordered pile of canceled checks. I squatted down and reached for it. It was damp, as if it had recently been pulled out of the print washer.

The picture was of The Tidepools. It must have been taken on a day when it was going to storm, because there were dark clouds in the sky and the trees looked bent from a strong wind. It was a haunting photo and artistically I could appreciate it—but I couldn't for the life of me figure out what it was doing here in the living room.

After studying it for a moment, I looked up at the stairway, then went back to the darkroom.

The other prints in the washer were similar—all of The Tidepools and all taken on the same storm-threatening day. They told me nothing. Neither did the photos that were spilled out on the floor. They were all of Snelling's clients, many of whom I recognized as celebrities. Finally I went back to the door, shut it and put out the lights, and then found the switch on the enlarger.

The image of the negative in the holder blazed up on the board beneath the lens. It was out of focus and, after some fumbling, I corrected it. Since the blacks and whites were reversed, it would have been difficult for anyone who couldn't read negatives to distinguish who the people were.

A bearded, dark-haired Abe Snelling—Andy Smith, as he had been known then—stood with his arms around two women. One was Susan Tellenberg; the other I had never seen before, but I guessed it was Barbara Smith. She bore a close resemblance to her sister. In the background, I could make out a cypress grove, probably one of those on the grounds at The Tidepools.

So what did all of this tell me? That Snelling had been taking a nostalgic look at his past?

I took the holder out of the enlarger and examined the other negatives on the strip. They were variations of the same pose. I wondered who had held the camera or if Snelling had used a timing device and jumped into the picture at the last second. But did it matter? The negatives told me nothing except what the dead woman had looked like. I reached under the edge of the light table and felt for a switch so I could see what else Snelling had been working on.

The white Plexiglas glowed softly. A magnifying loupe lay to one side, and I picked it up so I could see the negatives more clearly. In one of the protective plastic sheets there were more of The Tidepools and more of Susan and Barbara. Snelling must have taken his camera when he fled Port San Marco, with this roll of film inside it. I turned to the other plastic holder. In it were scenes of San Francisco. I leaned over them with interest, realizing one was the negative of the photo that had made Snelling famous.

There, in reverse black-and-white, was the anguished face of the restaurant proprietor's wife. And the still face of her husband. There were twelve shots that must have been taken in rapid succession, and I marveled at how Snelling had known exactly which one to pick to give him that essential quality of pain and horror.

But there were more shots that had been taken that day. Shots that, by the sequence of the numbers printed on the film, had been taken before these. They showed the rest of the cafe, the striped umbrellas, the little flowers in vases on the tables.

And they showed another face I recognized.

I stared down, gripping the edges of the light table. That face was the reason Snelling had stopped at the Blue Owl that day and inadvertently become famous.

I didn't have time to search Snelling's files for prints of these, and I was fairly certain they wouldn't be there anyway. The person who had ransacked the house would have taken them. But the negatives lying on the light table hadn't meant anything to the ransacker. Someone unfamiliar with the photographic process wouldn't be able to read them or realize they were there because Snelling had been going over them, looking at them through the magnifying loupe, getting ready to print them. Before . . .

Before what?

I whirled and ran from the darkroom and down two flights to the lower level. I glanced into the first door off the hall and saw a bedroom furnished in light-colored Danish modern. Snelling's, probably. A couple of suitcases stood on the floor by the dresser, and a third was open on a chair. It was partially packed. I went inside and turned on a light. There was a thick film of dust—due to the nearby demolition—around it. The suitcase had not been packed today, and most likely Snelling had been taking things out rather than putting them in.

So he'd been prepared to run. What had changed his mind?

I left the room and hurried down the hall to the bedroom Jane Anthony had occupied. It was the same as when I had last seen it, except the phone book was on the bed, open to the notations on its front pages. I leaned over it, reading them more carefully than I had the last time I'd come here.

It leaped out at me, the final fact that made everything come clear. I would make a telephone call to confirm it.

But I was already certain I knew.

19

By the time I got back to Salmon Bay, I was physically exhausted. The tiredness I'd felt on the trip north was nothing to the bone-weariness I felt now. My arms and shoulders ached from steering; my right leg was stiff from pressing the accelerator; even my eyes burned from peering into the darkness through the headlights' glare.

But my mind was alert, primed by questions answered and suspicions confirmed—and by fear.

A dark green VW was parked near the end of the semi-circular driveway at The Tidepools. I drove past and left the MG several yards down the highway, then walked back and looked at the other car. It was pulled in at an odd angle, its rear end sticking out and nearly blocking the drive.

The Tidepools itself seemed unnaturally quiet now, at a little after ten. The front wing, where the reception area and offices were, was dark except for small security lights set at intervals under the eaves. They did little more than illuminate the juniper shrubs that screened the windows. Brighter light shone from the rear wings where the patients presumably were, but even these were filtered through a thin sea mist.

I hesitated, checking the gun in my purse, then went up the drive to the VW. Its door was unlocked, the window on the driver's side partly rolled down. In the glove compartment I found a registration made out to Abe Snelling at his Potrero Hill address.

As I'd suspected, Snelling had come to the place that—as indicated by the prints I'd found in his darkroom—had been very much on his mind all afternoon. And I thought I knew why he'd come. But where was he now? From the way he'd left the car, he'd taken no pains to cover his presence. But, then, he didn't have to; the people here had probably never heard of Abe Snelling. Even if they had, they would never connect the car registration with Andy Smith. And I was pretty sure Snelling had arrived in a hurry and not planned to stay long.

But when had Snelling gotten here? He'd left his house early enough for both the ransacker and me to search it thoroughly. And for both of us to guess where he might be headed.

I looked around at the three other cars in the driveway. Two were station wagons with the name of the hospice painted on their doors. The other was a new-looking Jaguar XKE. All three cars had been in the drive on my previous visits.

Slipping into a grove of eucalyptus that bordered the right side of the driveway, I studied the low-shingled building. It was cold, and a strong wind blew off the ocean, rattling the dry leaves above my head. I could hear the surf crashing on the reefs and when I looked over there I saw whitecaps billowing. The tide was starting to come in now; soon it would cover the narrow beach and batter at the cliffs. I thought of the sea anemones in their dark, icy pools, and shivered.

I stood very still and stared into the darkness, looking for a telltale movement among the trees. Snelling had to be here some place—but where? Perhaps I should have gone directly to the police and let them find him. But what did I really have to tell them? Only that I felt, because I'd read Snelling's negatives, it was all going to end here, where it had begun?

No, it would have taken the police—skeptical as they were of me now—all night to unravel my cat's cradle of suspicions. And even then, I was afraid they would not take me seriously. Besides, this was my investigation; I should be the one to wrap it up.

I began to circle the buildings counterclockwise, keeping under the trees. The wind blew stronger and colder as I moved toward the sea. Through the rustle of the leaves and the scraping of branches, I could make out the strains of classical music. I followed them to a brightly lit side window and looked in from my dark vantage point. The window opened onto a large living room, full of comfortable, overstuffed furniture. A string quartet—three men and a woman—was playing on a raised platform at the front of the room, and about ten people sat listening. I tried to think of what the piece was. Mozart, maybe. Don would know. Don . . .

I stepped farther back into the shadows and continued circling. At the rear of the complex was a series of ells with sliding glass doors that reminded me of a motel. This was probably where the patients' rooms were. There were a number of lights on and through one door I saw a white-haired man sitting up in bed reading. Yes, these were the living quarters.

What was left? I turned and surveyed the grounds. There was a small shingled outbuilding closer to the cliff's edge. I started over there, sprinting across an open stretch of lawn and into a clump of wind-bent cypress. They were more thickly planted than the eucalyptus and, before my eyes could adjust to the blackness, a low-hanging branch caught me square in the face. I swatted at it and then felt my cheek. It was scratched, but only superficially.

Stand still until you can see where you're going, dummy, I told myself.

I waited there, listening to the roar of the surf, until I could make out the shapes of the individual trees. Snelling, I thought. Where the devil was Snelling?

A movement off to my right caught my eye. I whirled and looked over, but it was only a curtain being pulled across one of the sliding glass doors. Its light-colored panels fluttered into place and became still.

I turned back and began scaling the rocky terrain under the cypress to where it sloped down toward the cliff's edge. There the ground dropped abruptly away to the jagged reefs. The tide was coming in fast now, white water boiling around the dark outcroppings. The wind blew steadily, and I gripped a tree trunk for support.

The outbuilding was some fifty feet away, across a

strip of open lawn. Once on the grass, I would be silhouetted against the horizon and easily spotted from any of the hospice's wings. I debated chancing it, decided not to, and instead peered over there, trying to see what the building was. In the same architectural style as the main building, it had a peaked roof and small high windows. Its doors stood open.

A tool shed? These immaculate grounds would probably require the full-time services of a gardener. No need to risk investigating it. Although the grounds were not fenced and there didn't seem to be any excessive concern with security, surely someone would come out here if he spotted a figure prowling around a tool shed.

I went back through the cypress grove the way I had come, then skirted the other side of the main building. Lights in the patients' rooms were steadily winking out. I glanced at my watch but couldn't make out the time. Either they went to bed early here—which would be logical, since the place was a sort of hospital—or I'd been moving through the trees for longer than I'd realized. I slipped forward to the edge of the foliage, where the mist-shrouded moon provided some illumination. The hands of my watch showed ten-twenty.

I'd been here nearly fifteen minutes and hadn't spotted Snelling. Where was he?

In the closest room of the bedroom wing, about twenty feet away from me, the glass door slid open. I stepped back. The tree branches rustled.

"Over there," a man's voice said. "I could swear I saw someone."

"Where?" The second voice was female.

"Under those trees. Someone was standing right at the edge, watching the place."

"I don't see anyone."

"They moved back when I opened the door. You could see the branches shake, couldn't you? Someone's hiding out there."

"Why would anyone do that?" The woman's voice was patient and somehow patronizing. A nurse, I thought.

"How should I know? But I saw someone. For all we know, they're casing the place."

"Why?" This time there was an edge of annoyance to the word.

"I don't know! Drugs, maybe. Someone looking to steal drugs."

"Well, it won't do him any good no matter how hard he 'cases.' The drugs are under lock and key and only the pharmacist can open up. And I think now it's time you went to bed."

"I tell you, I saw someone."

"There's no one out there."

"Just you wait until you're sitting out there at the nurses' station and some crazed hophead bursts in and pulls a gun on you and tries to make you open up the pharmacy. Don't say I didn't warn—" The door slammed shut.

I moved deeper into the grove of trees and waited a full five minutes before I moved on. While the nurse claimed not to believe the patient had seen someone, she might just have been allaying his fears. If so, she would send someone out to check immediately. Finally I decided no one was coming and made my way back toward the front of the grounds and the office wing.

Snelling's car was still parked at the end of the drive, as were the station wagons and Jaguar. I moved behind the juniper hedges so I could see into the office windows. Just then the front door slammed and high-heeled shoes tapped down the flagstone walk. I peered over the hedge and saw Ann Bates getting into the Jaguar.

The personnel director was here very late. Was that part of her regular duties or something to do with Snelling's presence?

Bates stopped, her hand on the door of the Jaguar. Then she turned and went down the drive to Snelling's car. She looked it over without trying its doors. Then she shrugged and went back to her sports car.

So much for the idea that Snelling had confronted Bates, I thought. If the personnel director hadn't seen him, then where *was* he?

The Jaguar's engine roared and its lights flashed on. It swung up the semicircle, beams sweeping over the facade of the building—and over the bush in front of me. I ducked, unsure whether I'd moved in time. The car continued down the drive, red brake lights flaring briefly before it turned in the direction of Port San Marco. I crouched in the bushes, my heart pounding.

Ann Bates must be doing well as part-owner of The Tidepools, I thought. The Jaguar appeared to be a recent model and, even used, they weren't cheap to buy or maintain. No wonder she had caused so much tension at the hospice this past week; what with records disappearing and police and private detectives asking questions, she must be very worried that something would destroy her handsome livelihood. Perhaps that accounted for her late hours.

The conversation I'd heard between the patient and the nurse about a possible drug holdup had made me think about the hospice's security system. It would stand to reason there must be some sort of alarm. Even if the drugs were kept under lock and key, someone who didn't know that might force his way in and demand them. I inched forward, under the eaves, looking for an alarm box.

I found one, prominently marked with the security firm's name. A large warning proclaimed that an alarm would also sound at the Port San Marco police station. The wires running from the box were intact. There was no way Snelling could have breached the system. *I* couldn't even do it without the proper tools—and I knew a fair amount about burglar alarms from my days in security work.

The only place I hadn't checked was the tool shed. And come to think of it, what was its door doing open anyway?

I hurried back through the trees, past the bedroom wing. Almost all the lights were off there now.

Into the cypress grove, down toward the sea. This time I was careful not to run into any branches.

The expanse of lawn looked as forbidding as before, but my motivation for crossing it was stronger. I glanced back at the hospice. The lights had been turned off in the living room. A soft glow emanated from beyond, presumably in a hall. Everyone was probably in bed but the night-time nursing staff, and I didn't think any of them would be standing by a darkened window. I ran across the lawn and flattened myself against the wall of the shed.

Breathing hard, I stared through the darkness at the hospice. No lights came on. No doors or windows opened.

Then I heard a groan.

It came from inside the tool shed. I waited, but it was not repeated. My hand on my gun, I inched along toward the door. Inside, to the right, was a lawnmower. On the back wall I could make out a row of rakes and hoes.

On the floor lay Abe Snelling.

He was on his back. The front of his light-colored shirt was darkly stained. But he was still breathing, shallowly, in ragged gusts.

I moved through the door, saying his name. He didn't respond. I said his name louder. There was blood, a lot of blood. Almost as much as when John Cala . . .

"Abe," I said, "dammit, Abe. Not you too."

I pushed my gun back into my bag and knelt beside him, started to feel for his pulse. A rustling sound came from behind me. Before I could straighten, something hit me from behind and I dropped the bag and my gun. Someone grabbed me by the shoulders and I felt cold steel against my neck.

"Don't scream," Liz Schaff's voice said. "Don't scream—or I'll cut your throat."

20

I froze. For a moment all I was conscious of was the icy blade against my neck. Its tip was sharp and pressed my skin. I was afraid to move for fear it would penetrate. It had done that to at least three other people. . . .

Other sensations returned. I heard Snelling's shallow breathing. I felt the sinewy strength of the arms that pinned me. I smelled the mustiness of the tool shed and the fragrance of Liz's perfume.

I tried to speak but my mouth was dry with fear. Snelling groaned again and I started to look that way, then realized the motion would put pressure on the knife. I swallowed twice, and managed to say, "It won't work this time, Liz. You've got a witness."

She laughed, an ugly sound like the cawing of a crow.

"He's still alive," I said.

"He's unconscious. Dying. I'd have finished him if you hadn't come across that lawn."

She began dragging me backward, toward the wall opposite where the lawnmower stood. Her grip on me was clumsy, one arm around my shoulders, the other lapped over it, holding the knife. Still, one quick jab . . .

She backed flat against the wall and we stood there in the dark. I could feel her heart beating fast.

I began talking, hearing my voice high-pitched and shaky. "Liz, you killed Jane and John Cala. You've almost killed Snelling. And now you want to kill me. You can't go on like this. You can't keep killing. There'll be more people who suspect, more who know—"

"Shut up." She shifted her weight from one foot to the other, forcing me to slump back against her. The pressure of the blade increased.

Still, she didn't do anything. We merely stood there in the darkness, listening to Snelling's breath, which now had begun to wheeze.

Was she waiting for him to die? I couldn't believe Liz Schaff had scruples about stabbing an already dying man. What had she been waiting for?

"Liz," I said, "I know about the women you killed at the hospice. Abe suspected, and so did Jane. It's only a matter of time before the police catch on. You can't kill an entire police department."

"The women at the hospice were different."

"How?"

"I didn't kill them. I procured drugs. They wanted to die."

"You mean they were sort of mercy killings." Cautiously

I felt backward on the rough board floor with my right foot. Her weight was mostly on that side.

"They *were* mercy killings."

"Did they pay you?" I moved my right hand slightly, to a small space between her left arm and the hand that held the knife.

"Of course. There was risk involved. I had to get the drugs from the pharmacy in town where I worked at night."

"How much did they pay you?" I shifted my weight to my left leg and tensed my muscles.

"Enough."

"Well, it sounds like killing for hire to me," I said, and shot my hand up through the small space between her arms. I knocked the knife away from my neck and kicked back with my right foot, circling her leg and pitching forward as hard as I could.

Liz stumbled sideways and careened across the shed. She slammed into the rack of garden tools and I heard something crash down on her. My bag and gun were lost in the shadows. I grabbed a sharp-pointed trowel from a shelf by the lawnmower, almost stepping on Snelling.

Liz straightened. She still had the knife. Its steel blade glinted in the moonlight that came through the small high windows.

"Put the knife down, Liz."

She stood there, panting.

"Put it down!"

She came at me, crouching, the knife extended. I thought she was going to try to come up under the trowel at my throat. Instead she dodged to the side and scurried out the door of the shed. I dropped the trowel and went after her, hurling myself at her feet like an NFL tackle.

She went down and I saw the knife fly from her hand. I crawled after it, expecting a struggle. Again she surprised me, jumping to her feet and running toward the cypress grove. I started to get up, but my foot slipped on the damp grass and I fell ingloriously on my rear.

Snelling, I thought, he's dying in there.

"Help!" I yelled. "*Help*!"

Lights began to go on in the main building.

"Help!" And I began to run toward the cypress grove.

The sliding glass doors of the building opened and two nurses and a man in a bathrobe appeared. They hesitated, then hurried across the lawn.

"There's a man in the tool shed!" I shouted over my shoulder. "He's been stabbed. Dying! Get a doctor!"

Ahead I could hear thrashing noises as Liz ran through the thickly planted trees and scrambled over the rocky ground. I plunged into the underbrush after her. My hands outstretched in front of me, I pushed branches aside and ran in the direction of the noises. If I could overtake her in here—

Suddenly my foot rammed against a big rock. My toe caught and I fell forward. I landed flat, struggled partway up, and fell again. The sounds in the trees ahead of me stopped.

Liz was already out of the grove, racing for—where?

I got up and went along more carefully, aiming at an

opening where the grove bordered the lawn. When I got there I stopped, scanning the grounds for Liz.

She was on the platform where the steps led down to the beach, the place where I'd seen the two old ladies sitting the day I'd gone out on the reefs to look at the tidepools. She was silhouetted against the horizon, looking back at the cypress grove.

I came out of the trees, running.

Liz whirled, first to her right and then to her left. She spun and plunged toward the stairway.

What was she doing, going down there at high tide? I thought. She couldn't run down the beach. It was under water.

I jumped onto the platform and rushed to the edge. Liz was halfway down the stairs. Waves slapped at the cliff, sending showers of spray over her. The bottom three or four steps were engulfed in the roiling water.

"Stop!" I yelled. "There's no place to go!"

She looked up at me, the wind whipping her cap of blond hair.

"Come back up here! You'll drown!"

She looked back down at the water, then jumped from the steps. I watched as she floundered and righted herself. The water, though turbulent, only came to a little above her knees.

I started down the stairway after her.

Liz plunged into the surf, swimming toward the reefs. A couple of the larger ones were still above water. By the time I reached the step where she'd jumped off the stairway, she was clinging to a reef maybe thirty yards away.

I jumped down into the icy water. The cold shocked me and I almost fell. Then I started wading into the sea, battling the waves for balance. The water splashed upward, each wave bringing a new shock until I could feel my skin turning numb. Finally I ducked under and began swimming.

I reached the reef and put out a hand for support. I could still touch bottom, but the current was treacherous. At any minute I might be swept off my feet. Liz, sitting on top of the reef, kicked at my hand.

"Give it up, Liz. There's no place for you to go from here."

She kicked at my hand again. I let go, and a wave sucked me under. Salt water filled my mouth. I bobbed to the surface, spitting and coughing.

When I looked up, Liz had retreated to the far side of the reef. Cautiously, I began climbing. The rough rocks cut at my hands. The knee ripped out of my jeans. I felt a trickling that was probably blood.

I pulled myself to the top of the reef and crouched there, panting. Liz was about eight feet away. Her hair was plastered flat against her skull and water dripped down her face. Her coat and jeans clung to her slight body. She stood with her hands balled into fists at her sides, her knees slightly bent. Weaponless, she was still dangerous.

I stood up. "Liz, there's nothing you can do. Come back to shore with me."

She laughed, a wild crow's caw.

I started forward, one hand outstretched.

She backed closer to the edge of the reef. One foot

slipped. She looked down at the swirling water, then back at me.

"Get away from me."

"No."

"I mean it!"

She lunged forward, grabbing my shoulders. Her hands went to my throat. I put my own hands up, trying to pry her fingers loose. They were as steely as the blade of her knife.

Liz shook me. "I mean it! You stop coming at me! They were always coming at me. Wanting something. All of them. More and more . . ."

My vision was blurring. I clawed frantically at her fingers.

"More and more and more. They wouldn't stop coming after me."

My knees sagged. I dug my fingernails into her hands a final time. The gray blurriness gave way to red and gold flashes . . .

Cold water hit my face. I groaned. An icy pool formed under my cheek. There was a second icy splash, and I groaned again. Salty water rushed into my mouth. I choked, coughed, and struggled to sit up.

I was lying on the reef, rocks cutting into my flesh. As I pushed up, they scraped my palms. I looked around, saw nothing. The surf was slapping higher than before, spilling over around me.

I looked down at where my face had been and saw an indentation full of water. A tidepool. I'd been lying face down in a tidepool. Liz had left me to drown as the water rose higher.

I sat up, looking around. She was no longer on the reef. Where had she gone? I couldn't have been unconscious long. Where was she?

I pushed to my feet, shivering with chills, and peered around. The white water spewed up over the reef, slapping at me and almost making me stumble. The stairway from the beach was half covered now. I could still make it back, good swimmer that I was, but the water would be treacherous. And I was so tired.

But Liz. Where . . . ?

And then I spotted her, on the only other reef that was still above water, many yards away. She stood there, her sodden clothing flapping in the wind. She was looking back at the beach, as if trying to gauge her chances.

I shouted but wasn't sure she could hear me over the wind and the surf. I shouted again, waving my arms over my head.

Then Liz turned. She saw me and shrank back, clasping her arms behind her.

"Get off that reef!" I screamed.

She shook her head, stepping backward.

I went to the edge of my own reef, prepared to jump and swim for shore. Turning, I tried one last time. "Get off or you'll drown!"

Again she made the negative gesture.

I looked beyond her and saw a huge wave rolling in. It was just peaking. It would break right where Liz was standing.

"Watch it! Behind you!"

The wave broke over her. I saw her tumble. The foaming water rushed on toward shore, but I couldn't see Liz anymore.

A second wave, even larger, was rolling in right behind it. This one would reach my own reef. I jumped into the swirling water and struggled toward the stairway.

21

When I entered Abe Snelling's hospital room, he was sitting up in bed reading this week's *New Yorker.* He was pale, and his eyes were deeply underscored with bluish semicircles, but otherwise you would never have guessed that two days ago he had been fighting for his life. When he saw me, he smiled and set down the magazine.

"How're you feeling?" I asked.

"Not bad. You?"

"Fine." It was the truth; I'd been staying at Don's since the night Liz Schaff had been swept off the reef and drowned. He'd encouraged me to indulge in wine, home-cooked Italian food, good music, and other pleasures. "I'm going back to San Francisco today for a trial where I have to give evidence, but I'll be back by the weekend. I wondered if there was anything you wanted from your house."

"Thanks, but my former sister-in-law already drove up and got me what I needed." He gestured self-consciously at an arrangement of home-grown flowers on the bedside table. There was another bouquet on the bureau—a lavish combination of roses and carnations. I looked at it quizzically.

"From The Tidepools," Snelling said. "Keller and Bates are probably afraid I'll sue because I got stabbed on their grounds."

I grinned and took a chair beside the bed. "The police told you the Coast Guard picked up Liz's body?"

"Yes. Lieutenant Barrow and I talked for several hours this morning. He's sure they can close the books on all the murders now."

I sat for a moment, silently reviewing the victims of those murders. Probably Abe was doing the same. Then I said, "One thing I wanted to ask you—did Jane Anthony figure out who you were by your photographic style?"

He looked surprised. "Yes. How did you guess?"

"I'm an amateur, but I've got an eye for style. Yours is distinctive; anyone who had seen Andy Smith's photos would wonder why Abe Snelling's were so much the same."

"That's what Jane did. She knew my work from when I showed it in little exhibits around Port San Marco. One day she just appeared on my doorstep in San Francisco. She recognized me, in spite of how I'd changed my appearance, and demanded I take her in, plus pay her a monthly . . . allowance, she called it."

"Blackmail."

Snelling nodded. "You know, when I first went up to

San Francisco, it never occurred to me that someone would recognize me from my photographs. I was always afraid I'd be recognized by my face. In fact, that's why I kept taking pictures—because I could go out on the streets and use a camera as protective coloration."

"What do you mean?"

"When you're holding a camera, people rarely look at you. Surely you've noticed that. They focus on the camera itself, or they get worried you're going to take a picture of them, so they start fussing with their hair. The photographer is just the anonymous figure behind the black box."

"Now that you mention it, yes, I *have* noticed."

"It was ironic—Jane located me because of my work."

"How could you stand to have her in the house, when she was blackmailing you?"

Snelling shifted and adjusted a pillow behind him. "At first it was awful. I even contemplated causing her to have an accident—slipping in the shower or something. But I couldn't. I realized that when my own wife asked me to help her out of her pain and I couldn't. I guess Jane sensed that and, as insurance, she wrote a letter about who I was, saying she was blackmailing me and that if she died violently I would have been the one responsible. She left it with her mother, to be opened in the event of her death. But it hasn't turned up yet."

"I doubt it will. Mrs. Anthony probably opened it and, when she realized what her daughter was, couldn't bear to show it to anyone."

"Probably you're right. Anyway, strangely enough, Jane and I became friends of sorts. The kind of relationship a prisoner and his jailer might develop. We used to cook together. We'd talk photography and I'd let her help me in the darkroom."

"And all the time you were paying for her silence."

"Yes. I think she was putting the money away, with some thought of helping Keller out of his financial mess."

"You knew about Keller?"

"Only that there was a boyfriend some place. I wasn't aware it was Keller until you told me on the phone a few days ago." He paused, his eyes clouding. "You know, if Jane and I hadn't developed that friendly adversary relationship, she and the others would probably still be alive."

"Why do you say that?"

"A few days before she disappeared, she was helping me organize my files. She must have seen the negatives of Liz Schaff at the Blue Owl and started to wonder."

"Why did you take those pictures anyway?"

"I recognized Liz as someone I'd known at The Tidepools and felt I should document her presence in San Francisco. But then the robbery happened and the shooting started. And, what with everything else that's gone on in my life since then, I forgot all about the negatives."

"And what Jane saw in them was the same thing both you and I noticed the other day—that Liz was wearing a pharmacist's smock rather than a nurse's uniform." I hadn't even picked up on that when I had had lunch with her at the Blue Owl, because it had been a cool day and she'd kept her coat on. "Jane must have remembered that

Liz also had a degree in pharmacy and had moonlighted at one while she worked at The Tidepools."

"I guess so. At any rate, she took off a couple of days later. And she did have Liz's hours at the S.F. General Pharmacy written down in her phone book, as if she'd done some checking."

"Do you think she knew Liz was in San Francisco before that?"

Snelling shrugged. "I think they may have had lunch a couple of times, but that didn't mean Jane knew she was working in the pharmacy until she saw the negatives."

So what Liz had told me about becoming worried when Jane missed a lunch date was most likely true, I thought. Only she'd been worried about her own skin, not her friend's. Probably she'd feared she'd let something slip at one of those lunches. "You hired me because you were worried about the letter Jane had left with her mother, didn't you?" I asked.

"Yes. I was constantly afraid something would happen to her—a car accident, anything—and then when she just disappeared. . . . Well, I had to know."

"But when she *was* killed, you didn't run."

"I started to. I packed my bags, but I couldn't bring myself to do it. I've been a recluse so long that the idea of going out in the world and beginning life all over again was just inconceivable. I decided to stay, and resigned myself to the fact that the letter would be opened and I'd be arrested. But then, the other day, when I started figuring things out, I actually felt some hope."

Figuring things out, I thought. Just like Jane had. "Once Jane verified from the hospice records that Liz had been on the team that had worked with all three patients who overdosed," I said, "it must have been pretty apparent to her how they got their drugs. And, since Liz still held a job and drove a rattly old black VW, Jane probably realized she must have salted away most of the mercy-killing money. So she decided to try blackmail on a larger scale."

"I wonder why the police didn't catch on to Liz in their investigations of the overdoses?" Snelling said.

"Probably no one knew about Liz's pharmacy job. The Tidepools, like most health-care facilities, must have fairly stringent rules against moonlighting."

Snelling nodded, looking tired now. "You think Jane set up the meeting with Liz on the old pier?"

"Yes. And when Liz fled after killing Jane, John Cala recognized her. But she also saw him."

"So she set up her own meeting and killed him too." Snelling lay back against his pillows. "At The Tidepools, in that shed, she kept ranting at me about how people wouldn't leave her alone. There she was, having killed all those people, and she was carrying on as if *she* were a victim."

"She was—the victim of herself." I was silent a moment. Snelling was tired and I should let him rest, but there was one other thing I had to know. "Abe, what exactly happened at The Tidepools? When did you get there?"

"A little before ten. After I left San Francisco, I drove down here and went to Susan's house. I had to ask her if she remembered Liz Schaff as being part of Barbara's medical team. I thought she had been, but I couldn't remember for sure. Needless to say, Susan was shocked to see me, but she did remember. She wanted me to call the police immediately, but I decided I had to verify from the personnel records you mentioned about the other women who overdosed. I drove up to the hospice, but there was someone in the office and, even if there hadn't been, the burglar alarm was turned on. Dumb on my part."

"And then?"

"I was on my way back to my car when Liz appeared, walking in from the road."

It fit with the time element, I thought. Liz had left San Francisco considerably after Snelling had, since she'd taken the time to ransack his house. "Go on."

"At first I tried to duck behind my car, but she spotted me. She acted friendly and said she knew why I was there, that she hadn't done the killings but knew who had. She claimed she had proof and asked me to come with her. I did. Dumb again."

"And she took you to the tool shed?"

"Yes. We were halfway there before I realized she'd trapped me. Then it was too late. She had the knife at my ribs. She forced me in there and started ranting at me. She carried on for I don't know how long and none of it made sense. Then she used that knife, suddenly, and that's all I remember until I came to in the recovery room here after surgery."

"You were lucky she got you into a dark place like the tool shed," I said. "She probably didn't realize at first that she hadn't killed you. And, by the time she did, I had crossed the lawn and she was afraid to do anything more than hide in the shadows. The darkness probably saved your life."

"No," he said. "You did."

I felt a flash of pleasure, followed by embarrassment. "I only wish it were that deliberate or well-thought-out. But, whatever, I'm glad you're on the way to recovery. And I'd better get out of here before you have a relapse."

He grinned wanly, and we agreed to get together once he got back to San Francisco. I went out and started down the hospital corridor, which was as starkly white as Snelling's living room. Halfway to the elevators, I spotted Susan Tellenberg. She was dressed in a crisp linen suit and heels, and her cheeks glowed as rosily as the basket of apples she carried. She didn't see me as she moved purposefully toward Snelling's room, and I didn't bother to call out to her.

In the lobby, I found a pay phone and called Don on the Hot Hit Line. We agreed to meet Friday night at the Sand Dollar; he had arranged to have the whole weekend off. Then I went out to my car and drove from the parking lot, toward the road that led through the hills to the freeway.

I flicked on the radio to KPSM and smiled as I heard Don frantically extolling the virtues of the local Black Angus Steak House. Then he did a traffic report, followed by a shampoo commercial. Finally he promised three terrific hits, back to back, no interruptions.

He dedicated the first song to me. It was called "Somewhere Between Lovers and Friends."

Also of interest:

Marcia Muller
Edwin of the Iron Shoes

A Sharon McCone Mystery

Sharon McCone, Private Eye. Single, scrupulous and sharp. She fights corruption and San Francisco crime.

When a small-time antique dealer is found murdered – stabbed with a bone-handled dagger from one of her own displays – Sharon McCone's first case begins. And it doesn't look easy. Her only witnesses are the shops inhabitants: Clothilde, the headless dressmaker's dummy; Bruno, the stuffed German shepherd; and Edwin, the little-boy mannequin with ornate iron shoes. McCone is determined to crack the case...but neither antiques nor people are quite what they seem...

Marcia Muller's first Sharon McCone mystery, *Edwin of the Iron Shoes,* introduced the world's first hard-boiled female private eye. It made publishing history and remains a timeless classic of the genre.

'Worthy of Chandler at his best.' ***The Sunday Times***

'Marcia Muller is the founding "mother" of the contemporary female hard-boiled private eye.' Sue Grafton

Crime fiction £5.99
ISBN 0 7043 4364 9